THE
THIRD
ROAD

Books by Martha Bacon

SOPHIA SCROOBY PRESERVED
THE THIRD ROAD

THE THIRD ROAD

by MARTHA BACON

illustrated by Robin Jacques

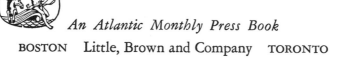

An Atlantic Monthly Press Book

BOSTON   Little, Brown and Company   TORONTO

For Kate and Erik

ATLANTIC–LITTLE, BROWN BOOKS
ARE PUBLISHED BY
LITTLE, BROWN AND COMPANY
IN ASSOCIATION WITH
THE ATLANTIC MONTHLY PRESS

*Published simultaneously in Canada
by Little, Brown & Company (Canada) Limited*

PRINTED IN THE UNITED STATES OF AMERICA

Carol

When all the beasts to Bethlehem
Were bidden by a sound
Of angels lilting on the air
First rose the lion from his lair
And shaking down his golden hair
Cried, "we to the Holy place are bound —
Up lioness, and come."

The elephants their trumpets raised
In thunderous salute,
The delicate deer with antlered brow,
The ermine shining in the snow,
Otter and ounce and geraboa,
The scale, the fin, the cloven foot,
Came, looked and loved and praised.

Then from her fire the phoenix spoke:
Shrill came her threnody:
"All fabled creatures, come behold
The myrrh, the incense and the gold,
Now bring your gifts a thousandfold,"
From Hy Breasil, from Araby —
They heard her and awoke:

The unicorns, all daisy white
With roses on their lips,
Sphinxes with riddles in their eyes,
Green gryphons, giants, atomies,
Mermaids and dolphins, swift and wise
Who frolick in the foam of ships,
All came that winter's night.

They with the morning stars did dance,
The creatures born of dream:
Beast angels, sweetening the sky,
Whose wide domain is fantasy,
Danced to delight Lord Jesus' eye,
To charm his ears, to praise his name
And do him reverence.

~~◆~◆~◆~~ ONE ~◆~◆~◆~◆~◆~◆~◆~

I AM BERKELEY CRAVEN, twelve years old and resident in the state of California. There are three of us, my sister, Roxana, whom we call Fox, because of her bushy red hair which she wears in a foxtail, little brother Caspar, who is nine, and me. This is the story of our summer in our grandmother's house. We had visited her several times in the past, but only for a short time, a weekend at the most. This time we were to spend a month.

We didn't know our grandmother very well. She is an actress. Actresses are not supposed to have grandchildren, and children tend to favor reassuring grandmothers with snowy hair and work-worn fingers. Our grandmother has even more red hair than Fox and her fingers are anything but work-worn, although it is only fair to say that she can cook when she cares to do it. She makes delicious chicken with artichokes, smothered in champagne and truffles; also a wonderful dessert of candied chestnuts. She is good at soufflés and dishes of her own invention.

To our grandfather we were almost total strangers. He had only recently married our grandmother when we came to pay this visit. He is an archaeologist and he digs up buried cities in South America. He was not as much excited by the prospect of three instant grandchildren as we might have hoped, but on the other hand we had not needed an instant grandfather either. However we became friendly over the food. We were never short of truffles, macadamia nuts, pickled mangoes, water chestnuts, and other necessities. Our grandmother kept cats, dogs, two donkeys, and several horses. There was a large garden to explore and the house was full of curiosities. There was a carved ivory chess set, there were jai alai rackets but no balls. There were peacock feathers in a Chinese jardiniere in the front hall and a huge, booming gong. There was an embroidery frame with a half-finished tapestry in it, a curious design of birds, beasts, and flowers, and there was a lute on the lid of the grand piano in the parlor. There was also a television set but it was broken.

The reason for our visit was to give our parents a holiday. Our parents manage a school — quite an ordinary school. By that I mean we don't do exactly as we please nor run about with no clothes on, and we have regular lessons. We actually spend our summers, as we spend our winters, in the school. Mother accepted the invitation at once, before our grandmother had a chance to uninvite us. She had said in her letter that she wanted to get to know us and Mother had accepted by telephone so that her mother would find it awkward to change her mind.

Father said that the experience would probably be broadening.

"I want to recognize them when they return," said Mother. "I don't want them so broadened that I shan't know them when I see them again."

"Your mother is basically harmless and she adores children — in her way," said Father.

"She isn't harmless and she doesn't like children. I was her child and I should know."

"Come now," said Father. "There's a great deal of good in your mother. She has her faults of course — everyone does — but — "

"Her faults are fine," said Mother. "It's her virtues that worry me."

"Keep your mind on her faults then, if it makes you happier," said Father.

"Perhaps the children will civilize her," said Mother. "Grandchildren sometimes have that effect, I believe."

Father began to harp on self-reliance and responsibility and quoted Mr. Kipling's "If" to us. I began to wonder how we should deal with our grandmother's mysterious and unfamiliar brand of goodness.

Of us all Caspar was the most pleased with the summer scheme because of the horses. He packed a red bandanna and the cowboy boots which he got for Christmas and said he was ready to leave. Fox took a more gloomy view.

"I shall be stranded all summer with two boys and nobody to talk to," she said. "There won't be another girl within miles. I don't believe Grandmother knows any families at all. She only knows actors and writers and people like that."

"What about the horses?" I said.

"I can't ride every minute," she said. "A girl likes someone to confide in."

"You don't have anything to confide," I said.

"If I had a chance to meet people, I should," she said. "But there I won't meet anyone worth knowing. I need people to talk about and people to talk *to*."

"You might be surprised," I said.

Our grandmother's house is about a hundred miles from where we live. It is near the sea and within view of Mission San Carlos Borromeo. The sea there is so cold that your teeth ache when you put your feet in it. The trees are shaped like demons by the wind and the sea lions shout down the waves from the offshore rocks.

In spite of Fox's gloomy predictions, we were all much pleased to be going to this interesting country, although sorry to be leaving our parents for six weeks. Caspar gave way to momentary tears at leaving but recovered once the bus got rolling. I myself had that feeling expressed by authors in the words, "little did they imagine what lay before them in the next twelve — or twenty-four — hours."

"Little do we know what fabulous adventures await us at our grandmother's," I said. "Here we are thinking it's just an ordinary visit."

"But you don't think that?" asked Fox.

"Yes, I do," I said. "I just said 'little do we know what fabulous — ' "

"Either you think there will be adventures or you don't think so," said Caspar. "You can't just sit there thinking little do you think. At least I *know* about the horses."

The thought filled him with such satisfaction that he complained of hunger, so we ate the chocolates we had brought along for such an emergency.

There is nothing to tell about our arrival. The bus station was hot and dusty, shaded by two scrawny eucalyptus trees. The prospect was unpromising but we had not come to visit the bus station. Our grandmother's gardener, Esteban, met us. Esteban is Mexican and we have become very fond of him. He explained that our grandparents had forgotten that we were to come today but fortunately he had remembered. He had come with the donkey cart because our grandparents had taken the car and the truck had been sent to town to fetch a new part for the generator. They have to make their own electricity at our grandmother's place.

"Your grandmother has much on her mind this summer," said Esteban, stowing us into the cart. "So much to do with the play she is acting in."

"What play is that?" asked Fox.

"The play about the Missions," said Esteban. *"El Camino Real.* Everyone for miles around is in it. I myself am the electrician. Conchita, my wife, is wardrobe mistress. Even that beast, my brother-in-law, is working on properties, ay-de-mi. Ah well, it keeps him out of mischief."

"Who wrote the play?" asked Fox.

"Brother Gregory at the Mission. All of us help him with our ideas."

"It sounds like an interesting play," said Caspar.

"It is," said Esteban. "It is full of action."

We wound along the road, catching glimpses of the blazing sea and the sea lions, their sleek, black backs shining in the sun. We passed the Mission nestled between the hills and the sea. A mare and her foal were grazing in a nearby field bordered with artichokes and one of the brothers from the Mission — we could tell him by his habit — was playing with the foal. Esteban waved to him and he left the foal and came over to the log fence and peered at us through the palings.

"Well, Esteban, what have you caught?"

He was a tiny man, not much taller than I am. He had a pale, pointed face, darting brown eyes, and a curious quick smile that brightened his features.

"Three fine fish," said Esteban. "They are the grandchildren, come to help with the play. How's it coming, Brother Gregory?"

"Ah, the grandchildren," said Brother Gregory. "How do you do and welcome, grandchildren. It's progressing, Esteban. It grows. I write it new every day. Things keep slipping in."

"When do you expect to finish it?" I asked.

"Ah, as to that — the actors will finish it, I believe. I can't finish it. I can't stop having ideas, can I?"

"No," I said, "I don't suppose you can. What is it about?"

"The Royal Road," said Brother Gregory. "This Mission — and all the others. Everyone that made the Royal Road from San Francisco de Borges to San Francisco de Assisi. All the people and all the birds and the beasts."

"You mean everyone's in it?" asked Caspar excitedly. "Even us?"

"Yes," said the monk, smiling. "Even you."

"But," said Fox, "I don't see how we come into it."

"You're on the Royal Road now," said the monk, "standing in the shadow of the Cathedral Mission. You can't help but come into it. They will perform the play soon and you will come and see it and that is being a part of it."

"Are there lots of costumes?" asked Fox.

"Costumes, scenery, music."

"Oh lovely! When is it to be?"

"Three nights from now. When the moon is full."

"Then we'll be going to the theater at night," said Caspar with infinite satisfaction.

"Yes," said the brother. He turned to fondle the foal who was nuzzling his sleeve.

"Goodnight, Brother Gregory," said Esteban. It seemed the moment to go. The little monk had dropped the conversation and had turned to the foal as though we had vanished and only he and the horses were left in the landscape.

We started away and the donkey picked up his pace, aware that he was going home, and we reached our grandparents' house after a half hour's ride. The house is called the San Exilio which means the Holy Exile.

I shall have to stop the story and tell about the house. It is a square Spanish house with a red tile roof and grills at the windows. It is very large; rooms lead into corridors with sudden little rooms appearing at the ends of short flights of stairs or around corners. Most of the rooms are not in use because our grandparents live alone here. Esteban has his own cottage on the place. But in spite of the emptiness the rooms are fresh and pretty. They are sparsely furnished with odds and ends of quite old furniture but they look as though they are ready at any minute to become very beautiful. They all have a view. The western rooms look to the sea and the eastern ones to the hills. To the south you can see the river winding through its sand to the shore. The northern windows all have a perfect distant view of the Mission like a scene in a paperweight. The main room is a kind of great hall with a fireplace at one end and a grand piano at the other and it is the only room in the house which seems fully furnished. Outside there is a grape arbor that winds down the hillside in front of the house, and there is an orchard of oranges and lemons and a few grapefruit trees behind it. Beyond the orchard lie the paddocks and eventually the wild country where pumas and eagles and coyotes live.

Esteban brought us into the house by the kitchen, a large airy room smelling deliciously of new bread. Our grandmother doesn't like bought bread so she bakes her own once a week.

"Make yourselves at home," said Esteban. "They should be back presently. I shall show you your rooms and you can look around. Don't go too far from the house."

We were content to wander about the house, upstairs to our own rooms and downstairs to the great room where shadows were gathering as the sun began to set. We touched the strings of the lute — they gave forth a sweet, mellow twang. There were two rough oak chests under the windows. They could have contained anything on earth — corpses, the wealth of the Indies, mysterious papers and maps. I tried the hasp on one of them. It wasn't locked at all — just there for show — and without really thinking about it I lifted the lid. Fox and Caspar gave a heave to it as well. A wonderful fragrance came from the chest: a breath of spice. Something far away and very old seemed to inhabit it. The smell came from the clothes folded there, a crimson mantle and a great skirt of silver brocade. We lifted the things out and held them to the light. They glowed in the rays of the vanishing sun, a persimmon-colored half disc sliding into the sea.

I put the crimson cloak over my shoulder and took the lute from the top of the piano and struck it. It made a stately sound. Fox, holding the silver dress in front of her, took a few formal dance steps. The door leading from the great room into the garden swung gently ajar, inviting us out. We put the things back into the chest and stepped out into the rose-garden, made our way through the roses to the grape arbor, past the turn-off to the driveway. Another path led to the orchard and a third one wound through a little thicket and led to the paddock.

This path rambled a bit and became quite narrow. We had to go single file. The trees arching overhead seemed suddenly very tall and the sea wind sang shrill among the leaves. Then the path suddenly widened and we found ourselves at the paddock.

It was a large paddock, surrounded by majestic live oaks and eucalyptus. Through the palings of a raw wooden fence we could see a string of horses grazing. Overhead an eagle wheeled in the sky. Everything else was very still. Somewhere in the hills I had the notion that the great cats and the little wolves waited with glowing eyes for the dark.

Again we noticed the wind. It came suddenly as though created by wings fanning the air and there was that odor of spices I had noticed in the chest in the drawing room. The horses were moving restlessly at the far end of the paddock. Then they wheeled and ran toward us as though intending to stampede the fence. They broke ranks halfway across the paddock and only one, a white one, continued on a straight course. He seemed huge as he pounded toward us at a dead run, coming on at ninety miles an hour. He was white as snow — or rather as the glaze on snow. His coat seemed to reflect light. His mane and tail were white but ended in darkness; his nostrils were

14

scarlet. The twisted horn between his eyes shone in the last light of the sun like an icicle.

I think we all caught hold of one another. I know that Fox's hand was in mine and I think she caught Caspar with the other. The unicorn crashed to a stop and stared at us through the palings as the other horses vanished through the trees.

We stood in a row and stared and the unicorn stared back. I cannot say that his stare was unfriendly, only fierce and penetrating. I tried to think of anything I might have learned about unicorns. Caspar had evidently tried to do the same thing.

"We're fighting for the crown," he crooned. "The lion beat the unicorn all around the town."

"My name is Guelph," said the unicorn gently. "I am the only one in captivity."

✦✦✦ TWO ✦✦✦✦✦✦

THE UNICORN had an interesting voice placed somewhere in the middle register — rather the lower end of it — and tinged with a foreign accent. Having introduced himself he stood staring at us with eyes which blazed like Catherine wheels. Presently he pawed the ground and tossed his mane. He was clearly growing impatient with us.

"I've done you the honor of introducing myself, I believe," he said. "May I suggest that it's about time for you to return the compliment. One likes to know to whom one is talking. People tend to be indifferent to matters of this sort nowadays, but I confess to being old-fashioned in this respect. We unicorns are inclined to be rather formal. *Autres temps, autres moeurs* and all that but it's difficult to change one's ways, especially at our age."

16

I interposed hastily and told him who we were. "Berkeley Craven at your service," I said, "and my sister Roxana. My brother Caspar."

The unicorn bowed gravely and said he was privileged to make our acquaintance. "And now," he continued, "where are we?"

"We're in my grandmother's meadows," I said.

"I see. And how did you get here?"

"We took the bus," I said. "It's the usual way unless you come by car."

"The question is," said Caspar, who had been eyeing the creature thoughtfully, "not how we got here, but how you did."

The unicorn tossed his mane a little pettishly. "I came by the usual way too. There is no question of a bus — whatever that may be. You must have come the same way I did. Otherwise we should not have encountered each other."

"What way is that?" asked Fox warily.

"Why, it's the third road, of course," replied the unicorn. "Fancy not knowing that! There is only one way from there to here — and from here to there. You must have come that way," he added triumphantly. "We all come that way — unicorns, gryphons, sphinxes, chimaeras. But the real question is not so much how I came here as how any of us came to be on the third road at all. One of you must have called me."

We vehemently denied it.

"Well," said the unicorn, "someone called me. The word of power was spoken — loud and clear. I was grazing in my favorite patch of asphodel and it drew me away and set me on the third road and here I am. If you didn't say the word of power, who did?"

"I haven't the slightest idea," I said. "And besides, what would they have wanted with you?"

"Oh, there are many uses for a unicorn," said Guelph. "We are in constant demand, actually. In matters of love and heraldry we are indispensable. We are summoned to preside over the discovery of buried treasure, the building of sand castles, and amateur theatricals. We know where to find lost poems and forgotten music. But usually we are given some notion of who is calling and why. A summons of this order suggests something of unusual importance."

"Someone's doing magic," said Fox.

"Undeniably," said Guelph. "Magic is certainly at the bottom of it. It always is."

"Since you're a unicorn, can't you do some magic too and find out who called you?"

"It isn't as simple as that," said the unicorn. "You see, I don't know what kind of magic was used. I don't know whether time magic or space magic was at work."

"In fairy tales," said Fox, "someone has a magic wand and it usually does whatever they want."

"Your fairy tales give only a faint impression of the limitations of magic," said the unicorn. "Magic is governed by its own laws and if you break the laws it can be very dangerous. For example, if you step out of the magic it is extremely difficult to return to it. This can be a considerable inconvenience if you should have left something in the magic which you might need."

"Like what?" asked Caspar.

"You might have left a near relation, or a piece of your past or even a few odds and ends of the future. Magic can be extremely treacherous. It can cause you to remember what never was and to forget what might have been or even what is. You can never be sure how it will behave."

"Well, we must certainly find out who sent for you," said Fox. "Perhaps they need you badly. Their father is going to marry them off to a horrid old miser and the beautiful prince has turned into a toad."

"Do such things happen frequently around here?" asked Guelph.

"Not very," I admitted. "In fact I've never heard of such a case."

"Things of that sort are uncommon in the best of times," sighed Guelph. "And to be quite frank, I was never interested in metamorphosis. I am a time wizard by taste and inclination."

"What's that?" asked Caspar.

"I work with time rather than space. I travel the rivers and landscapes of time very easily. I can take you to any time you please. Presumably this was why I was summoned. Someone had a definite use for a time wizard. Unfortunately I cannot return to Hy Breasil until I find who called me away. We must make the best of a bad business and start looking for the person."

"But I don't see where we are to begin," I said. "And I really don't see what it has to do with us. How can we possibly help you? After all we *didn't* call you."

"But there must be some reason why you found yourselves on the third road. You are bound to be connected with the call. Think about it, think hard. Unicorns have a thousand uses. They are good for lost causes, shattered hopes, misplaced affections."

He paused a little doubtfully. "I must confess that you don't seem to be suffering from any of these things."

"Not yet," said Fox. "But I expect we shall one of these days," she added confidently.

"Without a doubt," said Guelph. "In the meantime, you must help me to find the person or persons who called. The first thing to do is to let me out of here."

"That should be easy," I said. "We must find Esteban and ask him for the key to the padlock."

"Make haste," said Guelph. "I should not care to spend the night here. The first stars are beginning to show already."

"We'll hurry," I said.

"And when you return you must bring with you a garland or two of roses. I am conscious of the pangs of hunger."

"I'll fetch the roses," said Fox, "and you boys can look for Esteban." She vanished into the thicket in the direction of the rose garden.

We found Esteban sitting in his cottage over a glass of beer. He was pleased to see us and gave us both an enchilada to eat but he wouldn't let us unlock the gate.

"Why do you want to get into the pasture at this

time of the evening?" he asked. "You can't ride now. They'll be calling you to your supper. Your grandmother came in an hour ago."

I found that I was not able to give Esteban a good reason for letting us into the paddock. I might have explained that there was a unicorn who had got there by mistake and that he wanted out with all possible speed but this is not the kind of thing you can tell a grown-up.

"I shall take you to the paddock tomorrow and introduce you to the horses but I am through work for today and Conchita wants to go to the movies in Monterey. You wouldn't want to make us late, would you?"

"Oh no," I said, "but —"

"He won't like waiting that long," said Caspar.

"Nobody likes waiting. *Mañana,* little boy. *Mañana.*"

We returned in dejection to the paddock where we found Fox feeding roses to the unicorn through the palings.

"Esteban won't unlock for us tonight," I said. "He won't do anything until tomorrow."

"That is excessively disobliging of him," said Guelph. "Did you explain that you had a unicorn here in durance vile?"

"He wouldn't have understood even if we had," I said. "Grown-ups can't understand about you."

"That may be so," replied Guelph, "but I cannot be expected to spend the night in a paddock with a herd of mortal horses. Unicorns are notoriously short-tempered. I really cannot answer for the consequences if I am to be thwarted in this disagreeable manner. Esteban is extremely mulish."

"Couldn't we jimmy the lock?" said Fox. She produced a safety pin and handed it to me. I clambered up the palings to the top of the fence where the padlock secured the gate. I perched there and tried to turn the pin in the lock but it wouldn't budge. While I was poking at it Esteban came out of the woods on the far side of the paddock. I suppose he had been watching us for some minutes. Now he came around to put an end to our mischief.

"That will do," he said. "If you want to pick locks you had better learn to do it right. I shall be happy to introduce you to Conchita's cousin's nephew by his second wife. At the moment he is in jail. I ought to give you the strap, or tell your grandparents. The locks on this paddock are not to be tampered with. Is that clear? And look how you've terrified that gray. See how he runs."

The unicorn was running round the pasture: the

new-risen moon glinted on his flanks and his mane surrounded his head like a dark halo.

"Come along back to the house," said Esteban. He spoke kindly but quite firmly. I was in disgrace with him and a failure to Guelph who tossed an angry whinny after us as we followed Esteban toward the house.

Only an afterglow remained in the western sky as we turned into the house. The hills were gathered under the moon, silent and hooded. Our grandmother was standing before one of the windows, a cameo against the sky.

"You have seen the horses?" she said, as we came into the room.

We replied that we had.

"And have picked roses?"

"Only a few. I hope you don't mind," said Fox.

"Of course not. Provided you don't waste them."

"Oh no, we wouldn't waste them," said Fox. She looked straight ahead of her as she always does when she is lying. "I gave them away," she said.

The reply seemed to satisfy our grandmother. "I'm glad you have come." She came toward us smiling and the scent she carried reminded me of the contents of the chest. In a way she also reminded me of the unicorn except that she didn't talk so

much. Now she merely kissed us all around, rather
as though she thought she ought to do it than out
of grandmotherly exuberance, and told us to come to
dinner. She seemed on the whole pleased to see us
but preoccupied.

Dinner in my grandmother's house is a handsome
occasion. For one thing, her tables and chairs come
from a Spanish monastery. The chairs are choir stalls.
They fit us beautifully and we sit in them with
pleasure. The dining room looks out toward the promontory which is shaped like a lion's head and
shoulders. Usually we dine early enough to catch the
sunset during our meal and the sun flickers in the
wineglasses and they look like the Sangrail. Tonight
we were late and there were big stars over the
promontory. The candle flames seemed to mingle
with the stars and I began to wonder which was
which. Perhaps it was the wine. We are allowed

wine at table with water in it. I don't like the taste
very much but the idea pleases me.

On this first evening of our holiday, preoccupied
as we were with our new acquaintance and who
might have called him, we were silent at dinner.
Our grandparents seemed not to notice however and
talked animatedly to each other until interrupted by
Caspar who bowled his question into their conversation like a ball down an alley.

"What is the third road?" he asked.

"Where did you hear of the third road?" asked my
grandmother.

Caspar threw his liar's look around the table. "A
friend," he said.

> *Oh, see ye not yon bonnie road*
> *That winds aboot the fernie brae?*
> *That is the road to fair Elfland*
> *Where you and I this night maun gae.*

Our grandmother spoke the lines, smiling, as
though telling us a joke.

"Have you seen it?" asked Caspar.

"Yes, I've seen it."

"Did you travel on it?"

"Yes."

"Where did it take you?"

"Where would you expect it to take me? From here to there, of course."

"Of course," said Caspar. "That's what Guelph said."

"Guelph," said our grandfather. "Who is Guelph?"

"The friend I told you of," said Caspar. "His name is Guelph."

"And did you give your friend this interesting name?" asked our grandfather, smiling indulgently behind his moustache.

"No," said Caspar. "I expect his parents gave it to him. You don't name your friends, do you? They usually come with their names attached."

"That's a fact," said our grandfather, and laughed.

"At all events it's an unusual name," said our grandmother.

"He's a very unusual friend," said Caspar.

This time both grandparents laughed long and loud. "Straight from the Straits of Anian," said our grandfather and winked at his wife.

✦✦✦ THREE ✦✦✦✦✦

OUR GRANDFATHER entertained himself that evening by playing the piano, indulging in a set of stately melodious pieces, pleasant and soothing to the nerves. We felt it polite to listen but since he took no notice of us we left him and went to the kitchen, where our grandmother was making pastry. She allowed us to watch and offered some samples before sending us to bed. It had been in my mind to unfold to her the story of the unicorn but watching her, absorbed in her puffs and tricorns, I did not know how to open the subject.

When we went to bed, I mentioned my feelings to Fox who agreed that she felt the same.

"Nevertheless," she said, "we must rescue him. He can't remain in the paddock."

"But how are we to get him out?"

"We'll think of something," she said. "We must meet at dead of night by the paddock gate and let him out."

"Why the dead of night?" asked Caspar. "Won't we be in bed and asleep by then?"

"That's when people are usually rescued," I said. "Whoever heard of rescuing anyone in the morning? Or the afternoon, for that matter?"

"I think best at dead of night," said Fox.

"How are we to wake up?" asked Caspar, yawning.

"I shall wake you," said Fox. "We'll creep out to the paddock and conspire. This holiday is even better than I thought it would be."

"You thought it was going to be a total loss," I reminded her. "You said you wouldn't have any girl friends to gossip with."

"I never gossip," said Fox. "I don't believe in it. And I shouldn't have worried about a bunch of dreary old girls if I had known there was going to be a unicorn. You go to bed now, Caspar. If you yawn like that you'll break your jaw. I knew a girl who did that once."

Our grandfather's music was still sounding in the drawing room and over and under it I could hear the far-off booming of the sea. I fell asleep only to wake after what seemed a moment to hear Fox whisper, "It's the dead of night."

Fox can make herself wake up at any time she pleases simply by banging her head on the pillow the number of times of the hour she wishes to wake up. I only knew her to fail us once and that was when we had to get up early to keep an appointment with the orthodontist. But tonight she was dead on the mark. I heard a church bell strike two and I thought she had chosen her hour well.

Waking Caspar was like trying to rouse a hibernating animal. He was sodden and then vicious but he finally woke up. We dressed and stole down the stairs and through the kitchen, where a night light was left burning, and out to the paddock.

The moon was in the west now and there was no wind. All the countryside seemed frozen in a stream of silver. Beyond the headlands the sea puckered in the moonlight. The shining backs of the seals were touched with silver.

As we raced through the orchard to the paddock I began to believe that we were dreaming. There was no unicorn. A unicorn is a fabulous monster, a device on the labels of English products — but when we reached the paddock he was there, a sharp silver shape against the shadowy landscape.

30

"Now then," he said, when we were within ear-shot, "you are very late."

"You are lucky we're here at all," said Fox. "I thought our grandparents would never go to bed."

"I take it that your grandparents are persons of leisure and affluence. Otherwise they would have retired early in preparation for the morrow's tasks."

"They have no tasks," I said. "They do as they please."

"Splendid," said the unicorn absently. "And what have you devised to free me from imprisonment?"

"That is what we must talk about," I said. "Can't you help us with your magic? We can't unlock the gate without a key and the fence is too high to leap, so we don't know what to do."

"I suppose," said the unicorn, "I could give you the words of power. You could mount me and we could venture into another time. That at least would take us out of the paddock."

"But where would it get us?" I asked.

"Anywhere you care to go," said the unicorn agreeably.

"But we can't just go anywhere," said Fox. "We should be missed. They'd have the police after us."

"Let me explain," said the unicorn. "When you travel in time, the time you left remains as you left it. You won't be missed. They will never know that you have gone. The great thing is to find the place where whoever it was who called me from Hy Breasil is to be found."

"I don't see how we can even guess at that," I said. "It could be anyone, anytime, anywhere."

"There must be some reason why I am here," said the unicorn mildly. "Actually I know I am in your grandmother's meadows but where are they? When are they?"

"You are in California, the United States of America, 1970, A.D.," said Fox. "We are in a valley called the Big Sur, or near it. The nearest town is Carmel and I can't remember the pop. but it must be in the gazetteer. There must be a principal export too, but I can't think what it is."

"I have never taken any interest in commerce," said the unicorn. "This idle speculation is of no avail. We must take some action. Climb on my back and I shall give you the words of power. One of you must choose the time and place. I shall do the rest. You choose, little lady." He nodded at Fox.

"Oh dear," said Fox. "Oh dear. What shall I choose? I'd love to see . . . a princess, a princess in a garden with everyone bowing and everything she wants the minute she gives commands. I've always wanted to see a princess."

"Repeat after me," said the unicorn. Fox did as she was told. The words of power poured from her lips. It's no use writing them out. For one thing they can't be written in our alphabet. They aren't English or any other language. They are old words from outside the world.

We felt the unicorn rise in the air and the sky brightened about us.

We were beyond a doubt in a garden, a beautiful one. There were hedges and flowerbeds and a fountain leaping in the sun. The air was heavy with the scent of orange blossoms and there was a regular standing army of roses. The unicorn began to nibble them at once.

"Where's the princess?" asked Fox.

"She'll be by presently," said Guelph, with his mouth full.

There was a rustle of silk mingling with the plash of the fountain. We turned at the sound and saw a little girl standing under an orange tree. Her face was pale, her hair was pale, almost silver rather than gold. Her eyes were large and dark, and she wore the most wonderful dress I have ever seen. It was pale

gray with gold and crimson arabesques all over the huge skirt. She carried a black and gold fan, which she moved languidly to and fro, stirring the orange-scented air.

"Oh," said Fox. "The princess!"

I never saw anyone look so like a princess. She gazed at us with her large sad eyes and waved her fan, and we were suddenly embarrassed in much the same way that we are embarrassed by our grand-mother. I felt that someone ought to say something but I couldn't think what. It was Caspar who broke the ice. He made a little bow and uttered the follow-ing words:

"The princess, I presume."

At this we all bowed. It seemed the proper thing to do while we were thinking what to say next.

The princess seemed quite at her ease, undisturbed by our awkwardness.

"I am Margarita Teresa of Hapsburg, Infanta of Spain and the Indies. How did you get by the guards?"

"You mean we're in Spain?" I said.

The princess looked surprised. "Where else would you be?"

"Well, we didn't expect to be in Spain," said Caspar, in his flat way. "At least, not Spain in particular. We expected to meet a princess in a garden."

"I am a princess. This is a garden."

There seemed no doubt about this. The princess continued to study us gravely. I suppose we must have looked very odd and shabby to her, not at all what she was accustomed to.

"Who are you?" she said, at length.

"I am Berkeley Craven," I said. "This is my sister Roxana and my little brother Caspar."

The princess looked from one to another of us and then her eye shifted to Guelph, who was still nibbling the roses.

"What a beautiful horse!" she exclaimed. "Is he an Arabian? How white he is!"

"He's sort of an international horse," I said cautiously.

"He's eating the roses," said the princess. "I never saw a horse do that before."

"He's fond of roses," said Fox a little nervously. "I hope Your Highness doesn't object."

"Not at all," said the princess. "They're the king's roses. He has plenty of them. I myself am very fond of horses. They're my favorite animal. I am also fond of dogs. There is one of my dogs." She pointed toward the path and there was a curious little silky dog. "He is son to one of the king's spaniels. The king has many dogs. We are devoted to our pets in Spain.

"Mari-Barbola, Mari-Barbola, come and see this lovely horse!" The princess called to the weirdest little woman I have ever seen in my life. She was not as tall as Caspar but her head was huge, so large for her small body that she looked as though she must lose her balance and fall on that heavy head. She was dressed in the same fashion as the infanta, in a dark blue dress, trimmed with silver.

"Your Highness!" she cried breathlessly. "I declare Your Highness gave us the slip. Here she is, Nicolasito. Ah, Your Highness was suddenly" — she searched for words — "transported. Here, right here, Nicolasito," she called. A boy had followed Mari-Barbola, or perhaps he was a man. He was dressed as a man, but he was even smaller than the woman and, like hers his big face was old and his eyes sad.

"Your Highness moved with such extraordinary rapidity — " he managed to pay the princess an enormous compliment as he said this — "that we were quite outdistanced. Your Highness's cousin is in the garden to wait upon Your Highness's pleasure. May

I convey Your Highness's commands to my lord cardinal?"

"See this lovely horse," said the princess.

Mari-Barbola and Nicolasito turned to look at Guelph. They also saw us.

"And pray!" cried Mari-Barbola. "Your Highness!" She was clearly frightened.

"Holy Mother!" cried Nicolasito. "What are these beggars doing here? Be off with you or I'll call the guard."

"Oh no," said the princess. "They are doing no harm at all. Strange children they are, but better to look at than dwarfs."

"That may be so," said Nicolasito, offended, "but, with Your Highness's permission, that does not explain their presence nor justify the creature's eating His Majesty's roses. With Your Highness's leave I shall call the guard."

"No. Wait." The princess spoke so imperiously that the dwarfs seemed to shrink into the laurel hedges. In the hot stillness I heard the rustle of silk again and another personage appeared, a boy a year or two older than I, dressed from head to foot in scarlet. He was slender and dark with narrow eyes set close together and a large sullen mouth. He extended his hand to the dwarfs who kissed the great ring which glowed on one of his long, slender fingers. He bowed deeply to the princess who responded with a curtsy and then also kissed the ring.

"Cousin, I've searched for you everywhere," he began, a little breathlessly. Then he looked at us. "What have we here?" He shot a glance at the unicorn and then hastily crossed himself. "Cousin!"

"Yes," said the princess.

"Cousin, my eyes do not deceive me. Witchcraft!" He hissed the last word like a snake.

"I'm sure I don't know what you're talking about, Cousin," said the princess. "Where is the witchcraft? It it only three street arabs and a horse."

"That is not a horse, Cousin. That is a unicorn."

"Is it indeed?" said the princess. "I wasn't aware that it was, but now that you mention it I perceive it clearly. Mari-Barbola, observe, a unicorn."

"A unicorn," murmured Nicolasito.

Mari-Barbola crossed herself and said, "If it please Your Highness."

"Perhaps I should explain," I said, feeling that we had frightened everyone rather badly save for the princess, who remained quite unruffled. "We came here by accident. We didn't mean to intrude. It was just that my sister, Fox here, wished to be in a garden with a princess and so the unicorn brought us here."

"You admit," said the cardinal, "that it is a unicorn." And he made a curious gesture, holding up his index and little fingers like a pair of horns.

"We've never denied it for a moment," I said. "How do you suppose we should have got here without a unicorn?"

"You could not have got by the guards," said the cardinal, drawing his skirts about him. "It is witchcraft, admitted witchcraft. Who *are* you? How is it possible that such young children should be so versed in the black arts? Witchcraft! Veritable witchcraft."

"We're not versed at all," said Fox impatiently. "No black art about it. We only met the unicorn today by accident. And you ought to know that there's no such thing as a witch."

"It is palpable," said the cardinal, "that you yourself are a witch. You have domain over a unicorn. You deserve to be burned." He fumbled in his garments as he spoke and drew out a little furry object with claws on it. We looked at it with curiosity.

"Surely," said the cardinal, "yours is a most potent magic. Are you impervious to a badger's claw?"

"I guess we must be," I said.

"Are badger's claws magic?" asked Caspar, turning to the unicorn, who had stopped munching roses and was regarding the cardinal with amusement.

"Badger's claws never achieved anything," Guelph answered. "Recollect that we are visiting an era of darkness and superstition."

"You hear what he says?" said Caspar to the cardinal.

"We are an age of extreme refinement," he said huffily. "By what right does the unicorn make such statements?"

"In our time," said Fox loftily, "we don't believe in witches. We think it's barbarous of you to burn people who are probably mad and couldn't do any harm even if they wanted to."

"What do you mean by *your* time?" asked the princess. "Aren't we in the same time?"

"What year is it?" asked Fox.

"Of our Lord, 1660," said the princess. "It seems odd that you should not know."

"Well, with us it's the year 1970," I said. "Three hundred years make a lot of difference."

"I don't understand what you're talking about," said the princess, fluttering her fan. "1970. Are you implying that you are not yet born?"

"Or that you have been dead for many years," I said, not knowing quite how to break this news.

"We are not dead," said the princess, the cardinal, and the dwarfs all at once.

"But we are alive," I said. "We may not be born yet, but still — look at us."

"*Et in saeculo saeculorum,*" murmured the cardinal, clasping his hands. His brown skin had become parchment pale. The dwarfs bowed their heads. Only the princess seemed unafraid.

"What is it like in 1970?" she asked.

"Well, there's no king in Spain," I said.

"No king in Spain!" Her fan fluttered like a captive bird and she burst out laughing. "What will you think of next? And pray, who governs our provinces in Mexico? And our other colonies?"

"Treason," muttered Mari-Barbola. "No king in Spain."

"There aren't any colonies to speak of," I said. "They're all nations now. They have automobiles and freezers and movies and revolutions. They don't burn witches or heretics — at least not where we come from. And besides there aren't any witches. There never were." I thought I had better emphasize the point. I was afraid that the cardinal might set up a cry for the Grand Inquisitor. I had read all about this in *Westward Ho!*

"Do they have wars?" asked the princess.

"Yes," I said, "we have wars."

"With muskets and arquebuses?"

"Those are old-fashioned. We have tanks and mortar shells and atom bombs."

"I don't understand those words."

"Guns that blow up hundreds of men with one shot and flying machines that drop bombs which can burn up a city in one second."

The princess looked horrified. "Aren't you frightened to live in your times? I shouldn't feel safe in my bed."

"You don't anyway," said Fox. "You're frightened of sorcerers and the Holy Inquisition and the devil."

"How is it" asked the cardinal, "that these bombs you speak of are so powerful?"

"I can't explain it very well," I replied. "It's a question of splitting atoms."

"Lucretius and Empedocles defend us!" exclaimed the cardinal.

The princess drew her fan across her face. "How cruel your people must be," she said. "Spain would not treat an enemy so."

"Oh yes, you would," I replied, stung by her self-righteousness. "It's all in the books. Look what you did to the Aztecs and the Incas."

"Heretics and heathen," said the cardinal. "Only through bloodshed can they learn of the mercies of the Holy Church."

"I expect that's the way it always is," said Caspar, inexplicably cheerful. "Things are like that with us, too."

We had left the rose garden as we talked and we were now in a courtyard full of palm trees. Beyond the courtyard stretched a series of pointed arches leading to a palace. A group of ladies and gentlemen were assembling under the arches as though for a ceremony.

Suddenly the princess caught me by the hand and cried, "Back! Stand aside."

"What is it?" I asked.

"Their Majesties."

As she spoke a gentleman with blonde hair and sad eyes, very like the princess's came out into the courtyard. The lady beside him wore a black and silver dress, with an enormous skirt which surrounded her like a fortress. She also wore a huge curly brown wig with feathers and ribbons in it. Her cheeks were bright red with rouge. These two were attended by many dark-faced ladies and gentlemen dressed like them. All the ladies wore wigs and rouge and looked like marionettes. A man walked close to the king and talked with him. He was more simply dressed than the others and he was handsome with a friendly and gay expression.

The king and queen continued on into the court-yard. The princess, the cardinal, and the dwarfs bowed almost to the ground. Fox curtsied, and Caspar and I bowed. The friendly faced man glanced around the garden and then stopped in his tracks with an exclamation of surprise.

"Your Majesty!"

"Don Diego!" The king had seen the unicorn. I could tell because his face grew even paler. His big jaw trembled. The queen laid a trembling hand on his arm.

"Guards, soldiers! What deviltry is this?"

"No," cried the princess, "they're only children." There was a clash of steel about our ears. We were surrounded by dark faces, red and yellow tunics. I caught Guelph by the horn as he threw back his head, startled by the sudden noise.

I thought Fox was just behind me and I seized a hand. Caspar caught my other hand. "Got you!" he cried.

"Back to my grandmother's orchard in 1970!" I shouted, and gave the words of power, three times to make sure.

The sunlight, the flowers, the halberdiers were all gone. It was night. We stood in the orchard with the unicorn hovering above us. The cardinal stood beside us weeping, and Fox was nowhere to be seen.

Caspar and I looked at each other aghast. There was a silence broken only by the terrified sniveling of the cardinal.

"Well," said Caspar, "at least we got Guelph out of the paddock."

✦✦✦ FOUR ✦✦✦✦✦✦

FOX SHRANK BEHIND a clump of roses. There was an instant of intense excitement. Then Fox almost laughed. The halberdiers had merely presented arms, she supposed. They were standing stiffly in their ranks now, and the gorgeous procession was filing past her. Ladies swept profound curtsies, gentlemen bowed. The fountains threw glittering spray into the air and over its splashing she could hear the tinkling laughter of the little infanta. After the laughter died on the air, Fox continued to crouch by the rose bush, hearing now only the fountain. She stood up and looked about for the others. There was nobody to be seen. "They must have followed the procession," she thought and set off in the direction it had taken.

The garden was a large one, and after a quarter

of an hour of wandering Fox was uncertain of her bearings. "But the others can't have got far," she thought. "They ought to be looking for me." She turned into a small, formal grove of palm trees, peering about her for a sight of something familiar. She called her brothers' names, softly at first and then more loudly. She called Guelph. Nobody answered. The garden was empty — empty as the moon — although birds sang, water splashed, and a languid little wind rustled the foliage.

"Guelph!" called Fox. "Caspar, Berkeley!" Now she was angry and frightened, cold with fear in the midst of the sunshine and the flowers. If this was a joke, it was a very bad one.

"Are you looking for Guelph?" said a voice.

"Oh yes, please," she answered. "Where is he?"

"Not here," said the voice. "Gone."

"Gone where? Surely he hasn't left me here to find my way back alone."

"If he brought you here I expect he'll be back."

"Soon?" asked Fox hopefully.

"Who knows?" said the voice. "Sooner or later."

"Oh dear," cried Fox. "What do you suppose he's done with the others? And who are you? Where are you? *What* are you?"

"I am Guapo."

"I don't know who that is," said Fox. "I can't see you."

Fox looked up and down and around, but no one came into view save the small golden spaniel whom the infanta had pointed out — a very pretty dog to be sure, combed and shining and wearing a scarlet collar set with turquoises and bells. He was a dog in something the same style as the infanta; a dog who had been groomed until his coat shone like spun sugar, trained to ritual and dignity, and who never in his life had crunched a bone. His large dark eyes resembled those of the princess and the pale gold feathers on his paws were fine as Her Highness's hair.

"Here puppy, here puppy," chirped Fox, delighted and all but forgetting that she was lost.

"You needn't change your tone of voice," said the dog. "I understand you perfectly when you use ordinary language. Also I'm not a puppy. As dogs go, I'm fairly old — nearly five."

Fox stood staring with her mouth open.

"Catching flies?" said the dog. "You needn't be alarmed. I shan't bite you."

"I didn't know dogs could talk," said Fox, recovering the power of speech.

"They can't to most people," replied the dog. "Only to the ones whom Guelph brings."

"Why to them?" asked Fox.

"Because you have got outside time and can talk to anyone," said the dog. "I should have thought you would have noticed that already. You've talked to Guelph and to His Eminence and Her Royal Highness. Why not to me?"

"Of course," said Fox. "I didn't even bother to talk Spanish."

"All languages are the same outside of time," said the dog. "Travel is very broadening, don't you think?"

"I certainly do," said Fox. "I was never so broadened in my whole life. But I should like to know what has become of the others. I can't just stay here, you know. Where is Guelph?"

"I haven't a notion," replied the dog. "But I shouldn't worry. He'll be back one of these days."

"What do you mean by 'one of these days'?"

"Oh, in a century or two, perhaps. Or any minute."

"But I can't wait a century or two. Why, in ninety years I shall be an old woman. What shall I do?" And she began to cry.

"I shouldn't do that," said the dog. "You're outside of time, so a hundred years more or less won't affect you in the least. Guelph comes and goes. I've been on several excursions with him. He took me back to Egypt once and forgot me for years. I hunted lion with Rameses the Second and finally became a god. It was extremely enjoyable while it lasted, except for the cats."

"What had the cats to do with it?"

"I wasn't allowed to chase them. It was my only criticism of the place. Guelph finally brought me back here and for the most part I'm satisfied. Court life has its limitations. There is a good deal of useless ceremony and the cardinal teases me. Boys are much the same the world over, I suppose. But I'm devoted to Her Royal Highness. She shares her sweets with me and I flatter myself that if she loves anyone it's probably me. And then there is Brother Gregory."

"Who is he?" asked Fox.

"He's a good friar and the finest artist alive. He taught me all my tricks. And then there is Guelph from time to time."

"Can't you call Guelph back?" asked Fox.

"I didn't call him to begin with, so I'm afraid I can't. But sooner or later whoever called him will call again so he'll have to come for you. After all you're on the third road so you shouldn't be disturbed."

"That was how this all happened in the first place," said Fox. "We all came by the third road.

Guelph said so. Why can't we just catch up with Guelph?"

"You see," said the dog, "it isn't always easy to find one's way on the third road. It takes a bit of getting used to. Now why don't you forget that you're in a strange place and enjoy yourself. You could give Her Royal Highness a great deal of harmless diversion. You're something of a novelty and she needs novelties. She's very easily bored."

"I should say," said Fox, "that she's very spoiled and naughty."

"Let us not be harsh," said the dog. "Her Royal Highness has her difficulties. For one thing she is betrothed to the Emperor of Austria."

"At her age!" exclaimed Fox.

"Yes indeed. And I've seen royal princesses younger than she is bartered off for less than this marriage will bring. Poor princess! The only thing that matters to her is Don Diego — and me."

"Who is Don Diego?"

"Don Diego Velazquez. He paints us. He placed us outside of time. That is how I became acquainted with Guelph."

"But Don Diego doesn't paint Guelph, does he?"

"No, but Guelph is there when Don Diego paints. I can see him but the princess can't. Her mind's on Austria. Creatures like me can make free with time."

As they talked they had left the grove of palms and entered a courtyard which evidently served as a place of recreation for the court ladies. The infanta sat fidgeting on a marble bench under an almond tree, fanning herself. She seemed out of humor and the two dwarfs were trying to distract her.

"It was too bad of you to frighten the beggars off," she was saying. "They seemed amusing. If only José weren't so stupid. And where is Guapo? I'm sure the unicorn wasn't of the devil. He was very gentle and all he did was to eat the roses. And the children were so interesting."

"If it pleases Your Highness," said the dwarf, Nicolasito, gently, "one of the children remained behind. I saw to the matter myself. I found a means of detaining her since Your Highness seemed to find the strangers amusing. I trust Your Highness will recollect that her humble servant, Nicolasito, took particular pains to see that Your Highness was not disappointed of the entertainment which the strangers seemed to afford. Unfortunately I was not able to restrain the unicorn from a rapid departure, but I think if Your Highness will look toward the gate to the courtyard you will discern the red-headed child."

"Bless me!" exclaimed the princess, craning her neck. "Why, there she is. And I declare! She has Guapo with her. Certainly we are always grateful, Nicolasito, for the pleasure you bring us. Have we ever shown ourself otherwise?"

Nicolasito bowed and made no answer, merely stepping aside to allow the princess a full view of Fox in a soiled cotton dress and dusty sandals staring across the courtyard.

"Come here, child," cried the princess. "Let us see you closer."

"I'd do as she says, if I were you," said Guapo in a small voice. "And curtsy. That's what she's accustomed to."

Fox crossed the courtyard and approached the princess. When she judged herself to be within speaking distance she stopped and made a curtsy.

"Splendid," murmured Guapo. "With a little practice you should manage that nicely."

"Now tell us," commanded the princess, "where did the others go?"

"Oh dear me," said Fox. "I don't know. I've been looking for them everywhere."

"But they must have gone to wherever they came from," said the princess firmly. "Can't you go there too and fetch them back to play with us?"

"I can't get there by myself," said Fox. "The unicorn took them and left me here. I was sure that Berkeley had my hand but when they vanished I found it wasn't Berkeley's hand at all. I don't know whose it was. Perhaps I only thought I was holding his hand."

"It was my hand that you held," said Nicolasito.

"You! You mean you kept me here? But why?"

"Your company appeared to give pleasure to Her Highness," said the dwarf. "It was sufficient reason." He stood with his dark eyes fixed on the ground and pursed his lips as though he wished to say no more of the matter.

"Nicolasito is always most considerate," said the princess. "I have the greatest curiosity to talk with you and hear about your times. You are a girl? You look like one. But I expect you are dreadfully poor. Your clothes are very meager and terribly shabby."

"I'm certainly a girl," said Fox and added with some indignation, "but I'm not poor at all and my clothes are perfectly all right. They're what everyone wears. And I have two party frocks from Paris, France. I have an aunt who lives there and she sends me lovely things. And my grandparents are extremely rich."

Fox wasn't at all sure that this was true, but the

princess's grand assumption that she was a pauper annoyed her.

Fox's show of temper seemed to give the infanta great satisfaction.

"See how spirited she is," she said to the dwarf, Mari-Barbola, who had been watching wordlessly. "She is afraid of nothing."

"She has not had anything to fear yet," said the dwarf.

"And what should there be to fear?" rejoined the princess. "We shall not hurt her."

"Your Highness is invariably merciful," replied the dwarf.

"Should you not like to become a member of our court?" asked the princess.

Guapo gave a short bark. "Say yes," he urged.

Fox cleared her throat. "Your Highness is most kind," she began.

"Good, good," whined the dog. "You're getting the hang of it."

"But I must find the others."

"May I respectfully call to Your Highness's attention the imminent approach of Your Highness's distinguished relative, his reverence, the Grand Inquisitor," said Nicolasito.

"What a churchy family!" said Fox, half to herself. "A cardinal and now an inquisitor. Is he danger-ous?" she whispered to Guapo.

"I should rather think so," replied the dog. "It's his invincible ignorance. He can't help it."

"She doesn't seem to worry about him," said Fox.

"She doesn't need to," said the dog, "but look at the others."

Maria-Barbola and Nicolasito were making obei-sances so deep their heavy heads seemed almost to touch the ground. Fox thought she too would as soon not look the Grand Inquisitor in the eye. He was tall and slender and very dark with heavy eyebrows which gave him a look of fixed and heavy sadness. He was dressed in long robes of unrelieved black. He bowed to the princess and she curtsied in return. Fox thought it best to be on the safe side and curtsied too.

"At play, I see," said the Grand Inquisitor, curtly. "Ah well, it is best that Your Highness plays while there is still leisure to do so. I was in search of His Eminence. He is not with you?"

"Your Reverence can see that he is not," said the princess in her high, clear voice. "We were convers-ing together and he then took his leave. We have been alone here this half hour."

"Scarcely alone, I think," replied the Inquisitor. "I

perceive that one of the stranger children is still with you."

"She lost her way in the garden, I fancy," said the princess.

"The question is," said the Inquisitor, "how she got into the garden in the first place."

"Precisely," replied the princess. "That is what I am curious about. But she doesn't seem able to tell us."

"It should not prove difficult with sufficient persuasion," said the Inquisitor. "Now!" He barked out the word so suddenly that everyone jumped save the princess who merely fluttered her fan. The Inquisitor pointed a thin index finger at Fox. "Enough fooling," he said. "You were all in the garden together. With my own eyes I saw you — three children and a white horse. I presume it was a horse which brought you here. Where did you come from and where are the others gone to?"

"I wish I knew," cried poor Fox. "I've been trying to explain to Her Highness here. We came by the third road. If only I could find it I should go away at once, but I don't know where it is. I thought I had hold of Berkeley's hand. But I didn't. It was his." She pointed to Nicolasito. "We meant no harm. We only said that we wanted to be in a garden with a princess. At least it was I who said that. And I said I wanted a little girl to play with. So I got my wish and now I don't like it a bit. And besides, I only did the wishing. I had nothing to do with the way it turned out."

"You will have to explain yourself better than that," said the Inquisitor.

"If Your Reverence will refrain from frightening her," said the princess, "I think it likely that she will. Even the dog is excited. How can anyone explain anything if Your Reverence confuses everyone so? I assure Your Reverence that we were in the midst of a most friendly conversation. It promised considerable entertainment."

"Your Highness's addiction to entertainment — I can only call it that — should stop short of harboring witches and encouraging the freakish behavior of pets and dwarfs," said the Inquisitor angrily. "Why should the dwarf Nicolasito have detained the child? She says herself that he caught her by the hand."

"Better run," barked Guapo. "Better be off. Rabbits! Rabbits!" Fox bolted through the little arched gateway that led out of the garden. As she ran she was aware that something pursued her. There were trees everywhere and she threaded her way among them and doubled back, but she heard the patter of feet wherever she turned. She stopped in desperation finally and looked behind her. Guapo caught up with her, panting and shaking his ears at her.

"Don't run any more," he said. "There's no danger of the Grand Inquisitor catching up with us. Running isn't his game."

"Even if he can't," panted Fox, "he might send somebody who could. He seems to have lots of soldiers."

"He'll forget about you. That's the beauty of being a specter from another time. He'll fancy that you were nothing but a shadow or a rising wind. He'll go on nagging Her Imperial Highness about her imperial duties. She'll go on answering him back and neither of them will think of you again."

"But what about you? Won't they think it rather odd that you took off so suddenly?"

"Oh, I'm a dreadful little runaway. I'm always imagining that I see rabbits. The maids of honor say I'm the curse of their existence. If they're not combing me they're chasing me. I provide them with a great deal of healthy exercise."

"Well," said Fox, "just so they don't come after me. Where are we now? How are we to find Guelph?"

"I shouldn't be impatient," said the spaniel. "Guelph will appear in his own good time. He always does. As for where we are — we're in the middle of Madrid — the greatest city in Spain. We're in one of the poorer quarters. Even if you were stone blind you would know it by the smell. That's the trouble with these late Renaissance towns. You leave the king's palace and you find yourself almost at once in a most undesirable neighborhood. So different from the Egyptians. They were immaculate by comparison with these people. These hovels are inhabited by gypsies and they eat dogs like me."

"I should hope not," said Fox indignantly. "I shouldn't let them touch you. What a horrible idea! And, anyway, I shouldn't think you'd be very good."

"One man's meat is another man's poison," said Guapo, "and gypsies can't be particular. There isn't a great deal to eat in Spain at the best of times. However, if we should meet any famished gypsies, I shall count on you to assert that you plan to eat me yourself and to summon the constabulary in defense of your dinner. We're in the heart of their quarter and, since it's getting toward evening, I suggest that we hurry on. I have in mind to take you to the house of my friend Gregory, the Franciscan. He lives at the center of town, not far from the cathedral, in a more healthy neighborhood full of artists and pick-pockets and honest tradesmen and minor clergy."

"Gypsies know about magic," said Fox, pausing and looking around her. There was a strong smell of oil and fish and a constant ringing in the air. People were singing, talking, and playing instruments. The gypsy community hummed like a great behive.

"Tell your fortune, little lady, tell your fortune," cried a voice from within a cavernous doorway.

"Oh, if only you would tell me how to find the unicorn and get home," sighed Fox. "It's getting so late. They must be half crazy at home wondering where I am."

"You keep forgetting," said the voice, "what Guelph so carefully explained to you. They don't even know you're gone."

Now the voice ceased to be merely a voice and its owner appeared. Fox saw at once that she was in the presence of a gypsy queen of the first quality. The woman wore a heavy embroidered skirt of some purplish material shot with peacock colors. A short black velvet jacket with a gold fringe half hid a scarlet smock. Gold bracelets wound halfway up her strong freckled arms, and ropes of shining beads like intermingled drops of red wine and seawater hung round her neck. Two golden hoops dangled from her ears. Her hair was hidden by a kerchief with a curious design on it. The gypsy's face was sunburned and sea-green eyes gleamed under her heavy brows.

"What will you give me if I tell your fortune?" she asked.

"I really haven't anything," said Fox. "I was hoping you'd do it free. All my things are at home."

"You could let me have your dog," said the gypsy.

"Oh, no I couldn't," said Fox. "He doesn't belong to me in the first place. He belongs to the infanta herself. I know the infanta." Fox could not resist revealing this fact. She had not met any royalty before and, now that she had managed such an important acquaintance, she wanted people to know about it.

"What would the infanta care? She can always get another dog."

"No, she couldn't. Not like Guapo. And besides he says that you eat dogs."

"I'm not over-fond of eating spaniels," said the gypsy, laughing. "But I'm glad to know that you won't barter the dog for a look at my crystal ball. It wouldn't tell you anything anyway. Come, have you any news of my lovely Guelph?"

"Oh," cried Fox, "I felt sure that you were just the gypsy queen I wanted. See, Guapo. She won't eat you. She knows Guelph."

"I'm not sure that follows necessarily," said Guapo. He had been making himself small in the shadows behind Fox but he now emerged into the comparative brightness of the gypsy's doorway. He looked the woman carefully up and down. "I'm not entirely persuaded that that's a gypsy. She looks more like someone's idea of one than the real thing. Gypsies are a greedy, thieving, dirty lot — and they eat dogs."

"You exaggerate, Guapo," said the gypsy mockingly.

"All spaniels exaggerate," said Guapo, as though he were proud of it.

"Tell us some of the court news then," said the gypsy. "Be sure to exaggerate it."

"Señor Don Diego is painting *her* in blue this time," said the dog. "Blue with a muff. Mari-Barbola has made herself ill eating quinces, and my lord cardinal has gambled away half the Indies — and won them back, if his lordship is to be believed. They will marry *her* to Uncle Leopold and she will rule over the Hapsburg lands."

"Poor dear," said the gypsy tenderly, "but it will be a lovely wedding."

"How do you know?" asked Fox. "It hasn't happened yet."

"I was there," said the gypsy disconcertingly. "All Vienna was lit by fireworks. They raised up Mount Etna and Mount Olympus and forged the wedding ring in the fires of Etna. White horses danced gavottes in the streets. The bridegroom was dressed in white velvet and diamonds, and he rode a silver chariot the shape of a seashell, holding a pearl in his hand, signifying the princess's name. When the Empire died they still remembered the wedding."

"That was her fortune, not mine," said Fox.

"Hers is past and done with," said the gypsy. "Yours is to come. It can't be told because you must find it."

"Oh dear," sighed Fox. "I'm sure I could find it perfectly well if I were home in my own century. But how can I find it here?"

"Just follow the third road," said the gypsy. "It will take you to it. The third road can only lead to one destination."

"But shall I like it?" asked Fox anxiously.

"You will like it very much. But you won't want to stay there."

"But how shall I get home from there?"

"If I were you, I'd attend to first things first. Remember you're on the third road. Once on it, you must follow it to the end. That is the only way to get home. Goodnight, child. Goodnight, Guapo. We shall meet again. Commend me to the sphinx if you go that way again. Also kindest remembrances to the plumed serpent, and especially of course to Guelph."

"Well," said Guapo, as the gypsy disappeared into the cave, "talk about spaniels exaggerating. She's no more gypsy than I am. She's on the third road most of the time, I'll wager. Since she isn't disposed to chat with us any more, we'd best be on our way. Brother Gregory doesn't live too far from here. He's a good fellow and it's quite a time since I've seen him. As I've observed before, this is a disagreeable part of town."

In this case Guapo was not exaggerating. The street down which they traveled had become so narrow that Fox could touch the buildings on either side by stretching out her arms. Savage women, toothless and haggard, lounged in the doorways. Dogs, cats, children, and pigs rooted in the rubbish, and bats lunged out of the gathering twilight at Fox's head, coming so close that she could hear them squeak. Somewhere in the distance bells chimed sweetly. They were very faint, almost as though they were ringing under water.

"Do let us hurry," murmured Fox. "I don't like

this place. These people look so angry. I hope your friend is really near."

"Just around the corner now," said Guapo. "Brother Gregory — he's a member of the clergy too, but rather different from the Grand Inquisitor. My man's an animal lover though he's fond of people too, if they're odd enough. He's saint Nobody, the venerable Nothing. I shall call him." Guapo threw back his head and gave a long, soprano howl. "Brother Nada! Span — Span! I'm lost in the wicked city."

A shutter rattled above their heads and Fox, looking up, saw a pale, pointed face gleaming out of the shadows.

"So, Guapo. You've run away again. This is no place for a dog like you. Wait now, while I unbar the door."

There was a scrabbling sound and the patter of feet running downstairs. The door opened inwards with a creak. "Come in, Guapo, come in. You will have to stay the night now. I cannot take you back to the palace until morning. They would never open the gates. Little girl, you should be at home. You had better come in too, lest you come to harm."

"Thank you very much," said Fox, slipping rapidly into a hallway almost too small to contain her, the dog, and the little man. He was forced in fact to back a few steps up the stairs as she came in. He pushed the door shut behind Fox and peered at her by the light of the candle in his hand.

"Bless me, child! You are oddly dressed. I wonder you weren't mobbed in the streets."

"We didn't go into the streets until it was almost dark. Please let me stay here. I'm lost. I'm on the third road but I don't know where it's going. Nobody will tell me, not Guapo, not even the gypsy."

"Ah, they often stay the night here when they've lost their way," said the man. "Come this way. Come, Guapo. Up the stairs. Good dog."

Fox and the spaniel followed the priest or monk or whatever he was up the staircase so narrow and twisted that Fox thought it a miracle the thing didn't collapse under their weight. Fox found herself in a long low room like a loft, furnished with a table, a chair, a cot, and a brazier. All over the walls hung pictures of birds colored like jewels, birds in flight, birds nesting, birds on the tops of steeples, and birds emerging from the cups of flowers. Some she recognized; robins and bluebirds and crows, and some were outrageous and outlandish, birds heard of but never seen. Laid out on the floor in rows there were pictures of animals, dogs, cats, horses, donkeys, and cattle and all manner of wild beasts, lions, panthers, elephants, stags, and even something which Fox took to be a giraffe. It had a long neck, spots, the body of a cat, and legs like a camel.

"Oh," cried Fox, "what lovely pictures!"

"I am a naturalist," said the man. "I have painted every beast God created. Unfortunately I have never traveled. When I meet someone who has been to a strange land I beseech him to tell me of the beasts he has seen. Those who have seen Africa bring me tales of lions whose manes are drenched with gold. See here how gold is the lion's mane. It is very expensive to paint lions. Once I hoped the Order would send me far away — but others went, not I. In the monasteries of El Dorado the brothers daily observe the flights of phoenixes, hippogriffs, and gryphons. And yet they complain. It is lonely, they say."

He paused and a faraway El Dorado look came over his features.

"I must make my bestiary without ever seeing one half of the creatures I paint. Sometimes I wonder whether some of them actually exist. Now take the mermaid. It is difficult to find anyone who has ever actually seen a mermaid. I have met several sailors who have known someone who has seen a mermaid and they were able to give me interesting descriptions. Unfortunately their accounts varied. Some suppose the mermaid to resemble a dolphin. Others declare it to be human from the waist up and fish thereafter. I have included both kinds in my bestiary. But I forget myself. Perhaps you are tired and hungry. Pray avail yourself of what there is. I have some bread, some wine, some olives."

Fox realized that she was hungry and though she never before had made a meal of bread, wine, and olives, she found it delicious now. The mixture of sour and bitter gave some sort of satisfaction which came, she concluded, from eating in somebody else's century. Guapo made a meal of bread soaked in olive oil and licked it up to the last crumb.

Their host watched them while they ate. His white, pointed face, with its bright mouselike eyes, gleamed out of the shadows under a painting of a stag holding a crucifix between its antlers.

"I have a honeycomb," said the little friar and he brought her a piece of honeycomb in a basin and put down a morsel for Guapo.

"Now that I see you," said the friar, "I perceive that you are dressed in queer foreign fashion but scarcely as a pauper. Perhaps you too will have seen strange beasts. You wouldn't have seen a unicorn now?"

"Oh yes, Guelph is a unicorn."

"Tell me, is he like my picture of him?"

He produced his picture of the unicorn which was very like Guelph save for the feet, which were like those of an elephant or rhino.

"All except for the feet," said Fox. "Otherwise it's a lovely likeness. Oh, I must take you with me. You'd love Guelph. Think of the picture you could do if I took you with me to see Guelph."

"Ah, the Order will never permit it, I fear," said the little Franciscan. "Brother Martin went instead of me. There he is in the land beyond El Dorado, watching his strange birds and the heavy-footed pards of that wild country, but for me — Gregory the Hedgehog — it cannot happen." He sighed deeply.

"Why do you call yourself Gregory the Hedgehog?" asked Fox.

"I gave myself the name after the pope who became a hedgehog, the only pope who knew how it was to be an animal. Sometimes I almost know. Guapo would tell me if he chose to talk."

"Ah, but he does talk," said Fox.

"I daresay," sighed Gregory, "but not to me. If I could find my way to Brother Martin's country, the loneliest place in the world, we might speak to each other. Not so, Guapo?"

"Oh, Guelph!" cried Fox. "You're so clever. Why *won't* you help us? If not for me at least for Gregory the Hedgehog." She stood up, stretched out her arms, and the words of power sprang to her lips.

⬥⬥⬥ FIVE ⬥⬥⬥⬥⬥⬥⬥⬥

THE UNICORN gave a long, subdued whinny. "That was a precipitous exit. You should give these matters more thought, young man. There seems to be some confusion about whom you are traveling with. Wouldn't it have been better to have brought your sister back here and left this other young person in his native habitat? Come, come," he continued to the cardinal, "I shouldn't take on so. You will encounter no harm here." The cardinal began to sob. "Aren't you rather large to grizzle like that?

"Ah well," Guelph sighed, "it's the unfamiliarity of his surroundings which are distressing him so. He'll accustom himself presently, I daresay. As for me, I was never more fatigued and we are no nearer our goal than before we started. Our journey hasn't even served the purpose of discovering who has called me. I trust you will refresh yourselves now as I propose to do. We shall pursue our search at a more seasonable hour."

I could see that he was extremely cross. "Wait a minute," I cried. "You surely aren't going to leave us like this! Fox is still in that murderous court. We must go back for her. Heaven knows what those crazy superstitious Spaniards will do."

"Since we shall pick her up at the moment that we left her," said Guelph, "they cannot do anything to her at all. And I am excessively tired. That trip may seem a little thing to you. Your only task is to utter the words of power, but it is I who must give them life. I wish you a pleasant repose. I shall seek a secluded glade and we shall meet anon." He vanished as he spoke and left us a scared little group in the moonlight. The cardinal continued to weep in a manner that would have shamed even Caspar.

"There really is no use in your making that noise," I said to His Eminence. "We aren't going to do you any harm and I'm sure that Guelph will take you home as soon as he's had a sleep."

"Suppose he goes off to sleep for days and days?" said Caspar. "What shall we tell Grandmother about Fox?"

"We'll say she found a girl friend and went to visit her," I said despairingly.

"Funny sort of friend that you pick up in the middle of the night," said Caspar. "And what are we to say about him?" He pointed at the cardinal.

"I don't wish to stay here," moaned the cardinal. "What is this place? You are witches and have brought me to perdition." He held up his badger's claw hopefully. He might have recollected that it did nothing for him in 1660 and it didn't do anything for him now. He cast it from him with an exclamation of fury and began to swear in a very lively and artistic manner. I've had my mouth soaped for far less and I am not a prince of the church. Caspar listened to him quite thrilled. Neither of us had ever heard anything like it. He eventually ran out of words and began to cry again.

"This is useless," I said to him. "You're perfectly safe here. You'd better come to the house and we will think what to do. It will be morning soon and some of us had better show up for breakfast."

"I refuse to stir from this place," said the cardinal. "I shall wait here until the beast returns and force him to take me to my home."

"That's all right with me," I said, "but if Esteban finds you here in the orchard he will probably send

76

for the police and have you locked up in jail. If you've any sense at all, you'll shut up and come with us. You can stay in our room until morning. At least you'll be comfortable and by that time perhaps Guelph will be ready to take you home again."

The cardinal looked like a trapped animal. "Very well," he sighed. "I seem to have no choice. But I can promise you," he added fiercely, "that if I come to any harm, the Holy Office and the secular arm . . ." Words failed him and he swept his hand across his throat. "Let me impress upon you," he continued as we scrambled through the thicket, "that your sister is a hostage at my cousin's court."

"And let me impress upon *you*," I said, "that you are a hostage here. And if any harm comes to her, you'll be sorry."

"Very, very sorry," said Caspar ominously.

The cardinal snorted and bundled his skirts tighter around his thighs. We made our way through the thicket in sullen silence and came to the kitchen door. It was locked, of course, and so was the front door. So, it proved, were all the ground-floor windows and the side porch. Finally we discovered that the little pantry window was ajar, and I thought we could probably poke Caspar through it. The cardinal and I, not without complaints from him, hoisted Caspar up and then shoved him through. Caspar complained that he was being cut in half but finally he disappeared. There was a thud and a slight splash, indicating that he had landed in the copper sink on the other side. Finally the kitchen door opened gently and we were able to step inside.

From the kitchen we made our way upstairs. Every stair shrieked as we tiptoed up but somehow we gained our own quarters without alerting our grandparents. I pushed the cardinal into my bedroom and switched on the electric light.

I should have known that he would have a fit. He gave a most unearthly howl. He startled me so that I immediately switched the light off again and then turned it on just as quickly. He screamed and Caspar raced into the room to warn us that we could be heard all over the house.

The cardinal flung himself on the bed and buried his head in the pillows while Caspar and I undertook to explain the light switch to him.

"It's nothing but electrical current," I said. "You switch it off and on. Only don't poke your fingers in the socket or it will knock you down — " There was no need to warn him. He lay moaning on the bed in an ecstasy of fear. It took half an hour to quiet him down. I thought I might calm some of his terrors by getting him to work the switch himself, but he wouldn't. He wouldn't even go near it. He just crouched on the bed, making the horns of the evil eye and hugging himself tightly in the eiderdown.

"You know," said Caspar, "he'll have to put on some ordinary clothes for breakfast. He can't come downstairs dressed like that. They'll lock him up in jail if he goes around in those clothes."

"It seems that one goes to jail for almost everything in this time of yours," said the cardinal. "Sleeping in orchards, wearing one's own clothes; it is all one to your authorities."

"You don't understand," I said. "It's not those things in themselves. It's what they mean. People wouldn't understand."

"What is that to me?" he exclaimed, and fell to weeping and wailing again. "Let me out of here. Where is that unicorn? How did this ever happen?"

I stood looking and wondering what to do next. There is no handbook with directions for what to do with a sixteen-year-old cardinal from seventeenth-century Spain overcome with panic in a twentieth-century bedroom. I did the only thing I could think of. "Shut up," I said, "before I knock your block off."

He gasped and sat up straight on the bed. He was

furious but rage had restored color to his ashen countenance.

"How dare you?" he stuttered, "how dare you address ME — threaten ME — a grandee of Spain. I shall send you to the galleys — the strappado — a slave market in the Indies — "

"There aren't any galleys. There aren't any Indies. We'll get you back where you came from as soon as possible. As soon as it's morning we'll wake Guelph. Believe me, I don't want you here any more than you want to be here. But you'll have to behave yourself until we can find the unicorn again. You'll have to adjust."

"I shall have to *what?*"

"You know, adjust, get used to it, fit in. I certainly hope it won't be for long. It shouldn't be but a few hours, but of course unicorns are funny. He might want quite a long sleep."

"What must I do to adjust?" asked the cardinal.

"What I tell you to do. The clothes, first of all. You can wear my best suit. It might be a little short for you; it's a little long for me. They bought it too large so it would last. You'd better try it on."

He scrambled into the suit with some help from me and looked at himself in the glass. It is a perfectly good suit — dark gray flannel — and he didn't like it.

"You certainly wear hideous clothes in your times," he remarked. "Do you really expect me to appear in that?" And he pulled off the jacket.

"It's the best I've got," I said wearily. "You had better wear it. I shall have enough trouble explaining to my grandparents why you're here at all. I've got to think up a story. We'll say we met you starving in the orchard and invited you to come for breakfast. They'll think it's awfully queer."

"They certainly will," agreed Caspar pleasantly. "They won't believe it."

"Think of something better then," I said.

"I've never been any good at lies," he answered. "People mostly don't believe me even when I'm telling the truth."

"I suppose we could even try that," I said, "but it will never work."

"No, of course not. What you need is a really good lie."

"A lie that has a little bit of the truth in it usually works best," I said. "But even the least little bit of it would sound like lies in this case. And we haven't even begun to think about what to say about Fox. Perhaps something will come to me."

With some difficulty we got the cardinal to stay in my trousers, which were too short, and to put on a red T-shirt. With his long hair and sullen expression he could have passed for any ordinary California person, beachcomber, activist, or hippie.

I took the robes which the cardinal had shed, cautiously made my way down to the drawing room, and stowed them in the great chest.

We whiled away the next couple of hours playing dice. The cardinal, as he explained, always kept a pair about him, usually tucked into his sleeves, and he had remembered to remove them when he changed his clothes. It turned out that he was a very good player and he taught us a number of interesting games. He liked to gamble and insisted that we start betting. We had very little money but we bet it all and he won it all — three dollars and sixty cents. The winning seemed to change his mood and he became more cheerful. Presently he announced that he was hungry.

"What do you eat for breakfast in your times?" he asked.

"Orange juice, eggs, bacon. Things like that. Muffins and marmalade."

"Will the servants bring it soon?"

"Our grandmother will call us. I expect she'll fix it."

"What very primitive lives you lead," sighed the cardinal. "Like charcoal burners."

I was offended but there was no point in quarreling with him after all we had been through to get him into a reasonable humor. At eight o'clock I decided to venture downstairs and face the grandparents. I met them in the kitchen, my story sticking in my throat.

"I know you'll be wondering about Fox," said our grandmother, "but early this morning little Margaret Hapgood came running over to ask for her. She's been waiting for a girl to play with all summer. So I called Fox and they went off together. I gave them an early breakfast."

I stood, as they say, rooted to the spot. My grandmother continued serenely.

"And I see that José has already come. He's been lonely too. What would you like for breakfast?"

"Whatever you like to make," I managed to say. "All your breakfasts are wonderful. In fact you make the best food in the world. And José is used to the best."

"Is he now?" My grandmother had set coffee to boil and brought from the pantry a bowl of oranges and grapes which she set on the dining room table. "Seville oranges," she said. "He should enjoy these." She began to create an omelet and told me to get a honeycomb, which lay in a covered dish on the kitchen windowsill, and put it on the breakfast table. There were thick-crusted rolls in a basket under a napkin to go with the honeycomb and fresh butter and heavy, yellowish cream. She finished her preparations for the omelet and walked out of the kitchen, leaving me fairly spinning. I was almost annoyed and began to want to tell her of our adventures, if only to get some reaction out of her. Why had she chosen to tell me such a story about Fox?

I heard her speaking in a low voice to my grandfather. I heard them laugh. Their laughter had a low pleased ring, almost like the hum of bees. What on earth was there to laugh at?

If my grandmother was the soul of discretion, I certainly was not, and I followed the sound of their humming laughter into the dining room and from there to the drawing room.

My grandmother had the cardinal's red robe flung over one shoulder and her brilliant hair fell half over it. She held up a crimson sleeve.

"Look, Berkeley," said my grandmother. "Did you ever see anything lovelier?" She held the robe against herself, smoothing it with her fingers, which seemed to act upon the robe like light. It glittered under her touch.

"Yes," I said cautiously. "It's beautiful."

"It will be the making of the play," said my grandmother. "Where would you find a costume like that — except here! Can you guess what it is, Berkeley?"

"It looks like what cardinals wear," I said.

"Quite so," said my grandfather, as though I had said something clever.

"He was a wicked little cardinal, and one of the swiftest dice throwers in Spain."

"What was his name?" I asked.

"José Maria Diego de Santa Eulalia y Valdes," said my grandfather. So that was why my grandmother called him José.

She laid the robe gently back in the chest after a few moments and said, "I shall take it to rehearsal today but it can remain here for the moment." Then she turned to me and said matter-of-factly, "Breakfast. I suppose you must be hungry. You had better call the others."

I called them and they came downstairs. Our grandparents greeted the cardinal with a grave good morning. The cardinal glowered but he was too well trained in manners to be rude. He bowed deeply to my grandmother and stood at attention until she had taken her seat at the table.

"What shall you do today?" our grandmother asked, when we were all served with the omelet.

My plan was to try to awaken the unicorn so I said, "We would like to explore."

"Where will you explore?"

I didn't know. There was a huge, wild country around us. We could begin almost anywhere.

"Go to Point Lobos," suggested our grandfather.

"What is there?" asked Caspar.

"Abalone shells, cypresses, seals. The skeleton of a sperm whale."

"I think we shall go there," I said.

"Or you might try looking for the Straits of Anian," pursued our grandfather.

"Where's that?" asked Caspar.

"Nobody knows. They're still looking for it. Or perhaps you ought to look for Hy Breasil."

Our grandmother laughed. "They're both waiting to be found, west of the western seas. There's a project for you. Don't you think you need a project?"

I said I thought we had one and she laughed again.

When breakfast was over we made for the garden. Fog was everywhere, clinging to the roses, dripping from the trees. The whole peninsula was wrapped in it. You couldn't see your hand before your face. I pereed through the fog, searching for the path through the thicket, but no amount of looking would reveal it. It simply wasn't there. There was no path.

 SIX

"I DON'T UNDERSTAND IT. It's not here," I said. "Let me see. We went through the kitchen garden — the orchard was over there —"

"The paddock's straight ahead of you," said Caspar, pointing. It was. I could see it dimly although the fog was thick as cotton fluff. The paddock was much smaller than I had remembered it, and the dark grove of trees beyond it wasn't there. I could see instead the outline of Esteban's cottage.

"Perhaps we came at it from the other side," said Caspar. But I knew we hadn't. Also I couldn't see a sign of the unicorn. There were five horses in the paddock all nibbling grass, none of them bearing a horn between the eyes.

I turned away from the paddock and tried to think.

I think best with my hands in my pockets. I don't know why. Fox thinks best lying on her stomach. Every time I thought of Fox my stomach turned over. "Gone to play with the Hapgood girl," my grandmother had said. Why had she said that? It wasn't true. I knew it wasn't true. I knew where Fox was. At least I had known a little while ago. Now she might be anywhere in time — anywhere at all. Suppose Guelph had decided to return to Spain and take her off somewhere else!

"We must find the path to the paddock — the other path," I said. "It's somewhere. It's just got to be here."

"Either it is here or you have lost your way," said the cardinal.

"He's right," said Caspar. "Paths don't lose their way. They always know where they're going."

I wasn't altogether sure of this but it sounded logical.

"Anyway," continued Caspar, "there's no use hanging around here. The unicorn isn't here. You can see that he isn't. I vote we go look for him."

"Look for him where?"

"Oh, anywhere," said Caspar. "He might be anywhere at all."

"Or at any time at all," I said.

"We might find him up in the hills," said Caspar, "or out on the Point or down by the Mission."

"Well, where shall we look first?"

"You decide."

"Let the dice decide," said José. "Double sixes we look down by the Mission. Double fours at the Point and any other combination we go to the hills. I shall throw."

He threw double sixes. I guess he had wanted to look down by the Mission. He pocketed the dice quickly and said, "Let us go."

So we went, winding down the hill through the fog toward the Mission. The pleasant sound of a barrel organ, playing familiar tunes, came to our ears. Someone nearby was grinding out the "Beautiful Blue Danube."

The sound was coming from an open field not far from the Mission and a little carnival pitched there. We could see through the fog the outlines of a target-shoot and lemonade stands and games where you could win kewpie dolls and cheap stuffed animals and glass cigarette boxes. There was a ghostly Ferris wheel and a phantom merry-go-round which moved to the sound of the "Beautiful Blue Danube." There was also a sign saying that the carnival was for the benefit of Saint Filomena's school.

"Look — a shooting gallery!" I said, and José, for the first time since I had met him, looked delighted.

"Weapons," he said softly. "I must try one." He was at the gallery at a bound, swung himself over the counter and helped himself to the nearest rifle.

"Here, you," cried an angry voice. "It costs money to shoot them things. Ten cents a round and get back over that counter where you belong." It was the attendant at the booth, of course, a red-faced boy a little older than José but not any bigger and he was mad.

I was anxious to try for one of the stuffed animals myself and began to feel in my pockets for a dime. José, paying no attention to the attendant, went on inspecting the rifle which he handled in a thoroughly professional way.

"Put that gun down and get out of here," said the boy angrily, "or I'll call the cops. What do you think this is? A free show?"

José deigned to look at him this time. "You had best keep a civil tongue in your head," he said coldly. "You are old enough to know how to address your betters."

He was holding up the rifle now and taking aim at the target. I could see that he knew guns as well as he knew dice. The red-faced boy leaned over the counter and said, "You'll put that gun down if you know what's good for you."

José fired the gun straight at the target and hit it dead center.

The boy vaulted over the counter in a rage and grabbed the gun. "Who do you think you are anyway? You heard me the first time." And he hit straight at José's jaw.

Our cardinal was afraid of electric lights and magic in any form but one thing that did not scare him was people. I don't believe that anyone had ever hit him before. The boy had not hit very hard; he was angry and the blow had glanced a bit, but it was enough to turn José into something like a cobra with rabies. He went white and put the gun down carefully on the counter. The he turned suddenly and made a long hissing noise as he hurled himself on the boy, threw him to the ground, and started to choke him. I flung myself on top of José because I didn't want the boy to be killed, and Caspar flung himself on top of me because he wanted to be in the fight, and all four of us rolled over and over in the dust and tore and bit and kicked until I felt myself jerked to my feet and shaken. Esteban loomed over me.

"You are impossible," he shouted. "Last night you

10 CENTS A ROUND

tried to let the horses out and now you're fighting. What's the matter with you? You ought to be ashamed of yourselves."

"We didn't start it. He did," said Caspar, pointing to the boy who minded the concession.

The boy plunged in with his account of José taking the gun.

"If he didn't have no money, he hadn't no business fooling with them guns," shouted the boy. "I'll have the cops on him. He's a bum, that's what he is."

"He doesn't know any better," I shouted. "In his country they don't have to pay to shoot. He never has to pay for anything."

"Well, that's some crazy country," replied the boy furiously, "and he'd better learn how to act in this one. He attacked me, he did. Assault and battery — that's a felony. Who is he anyway?"

"He's a cardinal of Spain," bellowed Caspar, before I could stop him. "And you have no right to hit him."

"I'll hit anyone who doesn't pay for his gun," replied the boy. "This here's a charity show, so it makes it all the worse. It's like robbing the poor box."

"I shall pay for the shot," said Esteban impatiently, "and you will come straight home with me before you get yourselves arrested for disturbing the peace."

"Please, Esteban," I cried, "let us stay. We'll promise to keep out of trouble. Just give us a little money and everything will be all right. José didn't mean to do anything wrong. He simply didn't understand."

"He looks old enough to understand," said Esteban. "Where did you pick him up, anyhow?"

"He — he came to visit," I said.

"Did your grandmother invite him?"

"She knows he's here," I said.

"If I give you money to see the rest of the carnival, will you promise that there will be no more trouble? I shall be here for the next hour, to see about renting their arc lights for your grandmother's play. If there's any more fighting, I'll take you home and lock you up for the rest of the day. I have enough trouble scrounging for this play without having to keep you out of trouble."

"Oh, I promise," I cried fervently, not thinking at all how I should keep my word. I had no control over José.

"Very well," he said. "Here are two dollars. You can all get a ride on the Ferris wheel or the merry-go-round and then the money will be gone. Then we will go home. You can help me with the lights. And stay away from the shooting gallery."

He gave us the money and left. The boy retired behind the counter and pocketed the consolation money which Esteban had given him. After exchanging a few sour looks with him, José consented to leave the guns and inspect the rest of the carnival. I caught his attention by explaining the Ferris wheel to him. He was delighted to know that it could turn itself round and round by an engine. "You have quite advanced entertainments," he said approvingly.

We found the Ferris wheel attendant and had a ride on that delightful machine and then, since the "Beautiful Blue Danube" was still lilting through the fog, we went in search of the merry-go-round. Caspar was crazy to ride it. We found it soon enough. The carnival was really very small but the fog had settled down so heavily that you could hardly see a foot ahead of you and the merry-go-round seemed to bloom slowly, like some great flower, out of the mist as we approached it.

It was a beauty of a merry-go-round with two rows of horses, white, black, and dapple gray, all gorgeously caparisoned, with rosettes on their bridles. They were in mid-leap on their shining brass poles and the merry-go-round was turning slowly on its axis.

As the horses wheeled around you could see glimpses of lovely landscapes, lakes, and flowering trees, and pagodas, and temples all painted on the inner column.

"I must have one just like it," said José, gazing rapturously at the spectacle. "My cousin would admire it. It would be the greatest marvel ever seen at the court." A splendid gray charger was galloping toward us and the cardinal put out his hand to touch the sleek neck.

"What a beauty!" murmured Caspar. "Almost as pretty as Guelph."

"Thank you, my little man," said the horse. "How is it that you come to speak of Guelph? I have an acquaintance of that name."

"Only listen to him," cried the cardinal admiringly. "To think that he can talk. You have marvels in your time. Veritable marvels!"

Caspar and I were far too surprised to say a word. José, however, had jumped to the platform in order to pursue the conversation and disappeared temporarily from sight. He reappeared presently on the charger, bending his head over the horse's neck in order to catch his remarks. This time Caspar and I jumped on the platform too.

"How admirably he speaks," said José, looking up. "Why didn't you mention that your horses are made of wood and can talk?"

"They aren't — we didn't know —" I began. "This is the first one we've ever seen." Our surprise was almost as great as his had been when he first saw the electric light.

"He says his name is Balthasar. I had a cousin named Balthasar," said José, bending over the horse again.

"How did you learn to talk?" Caspar asked the horse almost accusingly. "We've been on lots of merry-go-rounds but this is the first time we've ever met a horse like you."

"Oh, I'm a rarity all right," said the horse pleasantly. "I got here quite by accident and I'd prefer not to remain indefinitely. The work is pleasant but a bit monotonous. I was originally a sea horse."

This was interesting but it didn't explain anything. "How did you get out of the sea?" asked Caspar.

"I was frolicking on the shores of Hy Breasil near the Straits of Anian when I observed, running along the shore, a creature very like myself. It had not occurred to me that there were any horses living on land. There were differences, of course. He had four legs and his tail was of shining hair, but the most significant difference was the horn that the creature bore between his eyes. I hailed him and he came running to the sea's edge to meet me. For a whole day we frolicked among the rock pools and sea caves of the great promontory, and when night came we wandered inland so my new friend could show me its wonders. He showed me the meadows where the land horses graze and the cities where land people live and the saltless rivers which run down to the sea. We traveled extensively, I quite forgot to inquire where, but in the midst of our journeying something called him. He vanished and I was lost. I could not find the sea."

"That was Guelph all right," murmured Caspar. "Exactly like him — finds people, takes them places, and then disappears. He's the most careless animal I've ever known."

"It was careless," agreed the horse. "I wandered across the land, searching for the sea. It was a most painful journey. I was completely out of my element. Finally, I came to this merry-go-round. People were putting it together. There I was, just one of a large number of horses. They gave me a bridle with rosettes and a shining pole, and I have been here ever since."

It was a sad story and I said so. "How long have you been on land?" I asked.

"As near as I can guess, several centuries by my own time, perhaps longer. By your time, a year or two, I think. I don't complain, but I should like to see the unicorn once more. It gets lonely here and none of the other horses talk."

"Perhaps you can help us find the unicorn again," I said. "Lots of people want him. José here would like to get back to seventeenth-century Spain and we'd like to get our sister back from there. That's where Guelph left her. You'd like to get back to the sea again, I expect."

"Yes," said the little horse, "to the castle under the seas. Sometimes I can hear its bells, sometimes I think I see its towers in the air. But I can't find the road back. The Straits of Anian are very remote, and the road there has a way of disappearing."

"That's right," I said. "We're all looking for the third road." The Straits of Anian had a familiar sound and I remembered that my grandfather had joked about it at breakfast.

"Now that you have come," said Balthasar, "I hope you won't go away. It's such a pleasure to have someone to talk to. One gets extremely lonely." He ducked his head as he spoke and a tear rolled from his fine, glassy brown eye.

This was too much for Caspar who reached over and patted the horse's neck and said earnestly, "Don't cry, oh please don't cry. We shall never desert you."

"You are a most lovable child," said Balthasar. "Excuse this momentary weakness. Now that you have come, I feel convinced that this term of servitude must be ending. Clearly the unicorn is near at hand and we are all in the magic together. Otherwise we shouldn't be talking like this."

"True," said José. "But what an unkind thing this magic is."

"If you want rides," called a voice through the fog, "you must pay."

It belonged to a woman in a soiled dress with rollers in her hair. She didn't seem cross like the boy. "We aren't open yet but I'll let you have a ride since one of you's already up."

I gave her our dollar. "That's three rides each," she said, "and you get an extra one if you catch the brass ring. Here, sonny." She gave Caspar a hoist to help him up on a horse, and I got on another. Then she went to the central column and set the merry-go-round going in earnest. The music roared up and the platform began to spin. The horses flew up and down on their poles. We spun through the fog like ghost riders, round and round and round and round. José held himself high, looking proud and distant, and Caspar clung tight to his little black horse, glad, I think, for the safety strap around his middle.

The fog was so heavy that I could scarcely see the horse ahead of me and we rose and fell through the mist as though there were no ground beneath us.

I've always loved merry-go-rounds. I can forget everything but music and horses when I am on one, and this one was the best I had ever seen. I leaned from my horse, a white one with a gold bridle and pink and blue rosettes at his ears, and reached for the brass ring. I caught it on my thumb and sat back in the saddle, assured of my second ride. I could feel the platform accelerating under me and the pole rose and fell more swiftly. The motion became less smooth, more like that of a real horse. I could feel the body move between my thighs and his neck was warm to my touch. The white withers gleamed in the fog, and the dark mane blowing in the wind carried a spicy odor to my nostrils.

"Guelph!" I shouted. "You came back!"

"Naturally I came back. Or rather, I should say, I

never went away. But even enchanters must rest. I've just awakened. I slept well and I trust you did, too."

I couldn't help noticing that Guelph never thought of anyone until he'd thought of himself first, but I suppose that is how unicorns are.

"José here wants to go home," I said. "And I must say I think it was rather mean of you to leave Balthasar stuck on a pole all by himself for centuries. He's been dreadfully lonely. You can't think how glad he was to see us."

"I admit that it was careless," said Guelph, "but you keep forgetting that it all comes to the same thing in the end. I've explained and explained and you seem reluctant to understand."

"Oh, we understand," I answered, "but won't you please fetch Fox back right away?"

"I shall be delighted," said Guelph, "but since Balthasar, as you say, has been waiting for quite a while it seems only fair to attend to him first. Good morning, Balthasar, how do find yourself?"

"At the moment very well," replied the horse. "As you can see, I've found companions at last. But you've been a long time a-coming, Guelph."

"Why didn't you call?"

"I could not remember the words of power," replied Balthasar. "I could only hope that someone would speak them for me."

"Well, I'm here now. Where do you wish to go?"

The little horse was about to reply when José interposed. "I do not wish to go anywhere. I wish to stay with this marvelous — merry-go-round. I forbid you to return to Spain until I am ready."

"You were frantic to get there not more than an hour ago," I cried angrily. "You can't have changed your mind so fast. Aren't you homesick? Aren't you frightened of the twentieth century?"

"It is all so interesting," answered the cardinal. "I did not know about things like this."

"We've got to get back to Fox," I shouted. "The rest of you will have to put up with it."

"I won't go," shouted José. "I intend to remain right here — wherever it is."

"Take us to Spain," I ordered.

"Take us anywhere," screamed José. "Take us to the Royal Road of the Conquistadores, to the Straits of Anian, to Hy Breasil."

"Take us to Fox," shouted Caspar, and he gave the words of power.

·--· SEVEN ·-·-·-·

"YOU REALLY MUST TRY to agree among yourselves where you wish to go," panted Guelph.
"You've muddled the magic with your quarreling.
There is no telling where such a mixture of desires
will take us."

Guelph was moving at a gallop and a hot dry
wind struck my face and sand stung my eyes.

"It looks very lonely," I panted. "We must be in
a desert."

"So it would appear," said Guelph, shying as the
sand stung his flanks. "Considering your altercation,
we are fortunate not to have found ourselves in the
middle of an ocean." Guelph tossed his head and
sneezed, nearly pitching me over his head. I could
hear another horse gaining on me. José, on Balthasar,
cantered up, followed by Caspar on the little black

horse from the merry-go-round who was dancing, bridling, rolling his eyes, and snorting.

"I don't see the Straits of Anian or Hy Breasil or Fox or *anything,*" said Caspar. "Where can we be?"

"What is it? Where is it?" shrilled a new voice. Caspar's horse had evidently found the power of speech. "Where's my merry-go-round? Where's the music? Where are the prizes and the schoolchildren and the raffle tickets? What *is* this place, and who are all of you?"

"Now, now," said Guelph. "You're on the third road and I admit that it's an unsettling experience, but you're bound to get used to it. You're no worse off than anyone else. Calm yourself, dear colleague."

"I can't calm myself," said the black horse indignantly. "I'm not myself to begin with. I've lost my merry-go-round, my legs are tired, and I'm terribly out of breath. I suppose it's the same with you, Balthasar."

"I'm a little out of breath," admitted Balthasar, "but I'm delighted to find myself alive again. I feel that I'm on my way at last."

"On your way where?" asked the black horse.

"Back to the sea," said Balthasar, "to the Straits of Anian."

"You may or may not be," said Guelph, with

some asperity. "I confess that I'm uncertain at the moment of where or when we are."

José pulled Balthasar up, jagging him slightly, and said: "The Straits of Anian have not yet been discovered. Our holy conquerors are searching for them. One day they will reveal themselves and we shall claim them for Spain."

"What if Sir Francis Drake should get there first?" asked Caspar.

"A heretic and a freebooter," said José loftily. "He never found them."

"Neither did anyone else," I said. "In fact I never heard of them until our grandfather began joking about them last night. I thought they were something he had made up."

"I expect there's no such thing at all," said Caspar. "If they've been looking for them ever since your time," he nodded toward José, "and haven't found them yet, they'll probably turn out to be nothing but a fig-leaf of your imagination."

"Nonsense," replied José. "They lie far to the west and they wash the lands of gold. We shall find them yet."

"And Hy Breasil?" pursued Caspar. "Shall we find that?"

"Beyond the Straits surges Hy Breasil," said Balthasar, "the western islands."

"I don't like it," said the black horse. "I was dragged into it against my will. I don't see why it had to be me. I'm becoming more actual every minute and it hurts."

"Guelph says you'll get used to it," said Caspar. "Like having your ears washed."

"I don't wish to like it," complained the black horse.

"Aren't you being somewhat ungrateful?" said Guelph severely. "You may be about to see the great Straits and the shining shores. Few are so fortunate."

The black horse gave a plaintive little neigh. "I don't call that fortunate — a place which doesn't seem to exist. The way you talk anyone would think I'd won a trip to Disneyland in a raffle. We seem to be in the loneliest place in the world. What a chance!" he concluded vulgarly.

"The horses in your time," said José, "do not seem to have made very good use of their ability to talk. They do nothing but bicker."

"Don't blame it on our time," I said. "I haven't the least idea what time we're in."

There was indeed nothing to indicate what era or place we might be visiting. The great brown plain stretched in all directions to the horizon. There were rises which might have been mountains visible in the distance. Occasionally a candelabra cactus reared out of the sand. Our mounts proceeded in a leisurely manner, Guelph pacing majestically, little Balthasar, stretching his muscles and apparently enjoying the exercise, and the black horse dawdling. We might have been any three travelers observed at twilight or at midday or at the rising of the sun, approaching the gates of anywhere in the middle of a myth.

We passed a snake who reared up from a rock and stared at us with hard candy eyes. We reined our horses to look at him, while we stared, an eagle swooped down, caught the snake in his talons, and carried him up into the glaring white sky. Caspar's horse shied at the sight. Guelph resumed his pace and said, "We are coming closer."

Caspar leaned over his horse and patted his neck. "Eagles don't eat horses," he said. "There's nothing to be scared of. Tell me what your name is."

"Merry-go-round horses don't have names," replied the black horse sulkily. "And I'm sure I wouldn't know what to do with one even if I had it."

"There are a good many names suitable for horses," said Guelph. "You could be Man-o-War. Or perhaps you would prefer something more classical, like Bucephalus or Dobbin."

"Dobbin sounds like a cart horse. And the other is too hard to remember."

"You could be Whirlaway or Seabiscuit or Arts and Letters. They were all great racers."

"I've no intention of racing."

"You could be Black Beauty," said Caspar. "I've always liked the name. It tells you a lot about the horse, like what color he is and that he's beautiful."

"It's not original," I said. "It comes out of a book."

"I think it a very noble name," said José, "and it suits the horse."

The black horse plodded on for a minute or two and then said, "I like it. It somehow makes things seem a little better to be called Black Beauty."

"I thought you would enjoy a name," said Guelph. "It helps in what the twentieth century has chosen to call the identity crisis."

"Is that another thing that unicorns are good for?" asked Caspar.

"It is a little soon to say," said Guelph. "It is a comparatively new ailment."

The day had waned as we rode along and the hot breeze had given way to a cold one. The distant mountains looked larger now, and when I looked at

the horizon I thought I saw snow-peaks. Our horses began to move more rapidly and José suddenly rode ahead and then brought his horse up short before a cactus. He leaned from his horse and I saw someone crouched beneath the cactus.

It was a boy, squatting in the sand, clutching a small glittering object to his chest. When we came closer I saw that the object was a bird made of gold, encrusted with jewels and mounted on the shining coils of a serpent. The boy, an Indian, shock-headed, hook-nosed, and naked, fondled the bird and crooned to it. In the milky twilight, the bird seemed to burn like a brand from a volcano.

"Quetzlcoatl," murmured Guelph. "The plumed serpent. Eminence, beware."

The boy cringed under the cactus. José's eyes were glassy with greed.

"Give me that," said José. "I have come by God's command across the waters to take it. Give it me."

"No, señor," whispered the boy. "I may not give it to you."

"It is mine," said José, between his teeth. "I've come to tell you that your gods have died. Did they not promise you that they would die when we should come?"

"Yes, señor, they promised."

"Am I not the white god on the four-footed beast who should bring down the plumed serpent? Am I not what the priests foretold?"

"Yes, señor."

"Then give me what you hold."

"Señor, it is the body of a god."

"It is a dead body."

The Aztec bowed his head and clutched his prize all the closer.

"I must have the god," hissed José.

He leaned from his horse and caught the Aztec by the wrist, giving the boy a ferocious wrench. The Indian loosed his hold on the bird and José seized it and held it up. The light from a brassy moon streamed down upon the Indian's god, glittering on amethysts, alexandrines, opals, and agates. Far in the distance a wild animal gave a long catlike shriek.

"The jaguar," whispered the Indian and shuddered.

"I shall take it to Margarita," whispered José, fondling the bird. "She likes such toys."

"I shouldn't do that, if I were you," said Guelph briskly.

"But it is so beautiful," said José softly. "Our family has a great eye for beauty."

"Give it back to me," said the Aztec, his eyes gleaming angrily through a fringe of hair. "It is mine. It is *my* god."

"Your god is nothing but an idol."

"Then what do you want with it?"

"I want it for my pleasure."

"It will bring you no pleasure."

"Why should it not? I shall take it to my own people and they will delight in it."

"It will bring them no delight. It is not dead. It is the bird himself and belongs to our emperor, Montezuma of the Aztecs. It has brought him nothing but sorrow, but it is nonetheless his; and when it falls into the hands of others, it will carry his sorrow with it."

"Leave it, Eminence," said Balthasar, in a voice like a sea-sigh.

"It is always wise to consider the consequences of laying profane hands on the gods of others, however tempting they may appear," said Guelph primly.

"Give me the bird," cried the Aztec, stretching out his hands for it.

"No. I shall never give you the bird. It is mine now."

"Then neither the sun nor the moon will rise upon you. The stars shall hide at the sound of your name. Each man of your time who holds it will hold a theft in his hands. The bird is Montezuma's and can belong to no other."

His voice faded while we listened and then he was gone and we were alone on the plain. José clasped the bird, caressing its jeweled plumage in the moonlight.

"I do believe," said Caspar, "that we're getting somewhere. I hear bells."

He was right. Faintly on the air a bell tolled, and against the dark sky I could make out the outline of a squat tower or belfry. As we came nearer I saw a long, low building with a peaked roof. Except for the belfry, the place might have been a cattle shed. Beyond the building we could see animals, a few goats and a donkey. A little bonfire was burning just in front of the building and two people were huddled beside it. In the flicker of the fire I could see a third person. There was a glint of red hair and the flames, darting up momentarily, revealed a blue skirt. Fox was standing against the building, holding a little dog in her arms.

"Hush," she said, putting her finger to her lips. "They've forgotten all about me."

"Guelph," I said, "why didn't you tell us Fox was here all the time? You knew how worried we were."

"I think the least you could do," said Guelph loftily, "is to congratulate me on a superb feat of simultaneity, extremely difficult to achieve. You and Fox called me in the same moment. I was obliged to split into two and bring you together in the same instant. To be candid, I was not at all sure how it would work. I've had very little practice at such a maneuver. But surprise is, after all, one of the chief elements of magic."

Although my sister is a girl and I often find it necessary to pull her hair and otherwise keep her under control, I must say that I was relieved to see her standing there in the firelight, as real as her scuffed sandals and soiled dress.

"Fox," I cried, "Fox, we've been scared stiff about you. Why didn't you come with us? Why did you stay back?"

"Stay back!" hissed Fox. "Isn't that exactly like you! To blame me! It was you that went off and left me. If it weren't for Guapo and Brother Gregory, I expect I should be there yet."

"If you'd only kept hold of my hand," said Caspar, "we could have stuck together. As it is we've had to tell awful lies and pretend that José was a visitor and dress him up in Berkeley's clothes."

"What on earth did Grandmother say?" asked Fox, her curiosity getting the better of her temper and her relief at seeing us. I knew she must be relieved and so were we, or none of us would have been so cross.

"Nothing at all," I said. "She told us you had gone to play with a neighbor."

"That's funny," said Fox. "Because, in a way, I suppose I did. A neighboring princess. But only for a while. I met Guapo and he took me to Brother Gregory. And then suddenly we were on the third road and here we are. We did a favor for Brother Gregory and brought him to Brother Martin."

"It isn't a very nice place," whispered Caspar, glancing about him. The firelight flickered on the

dull adobe walls of the building, against which two
crouching figures were silhouetted. Dust rose from
the ground and seeped across the firelight. I could
smell it and feel it smarting under my eyelids, gritty
between my teeth. The dust softened and blurred the
outlines of the building and the people. It was hard
to tell where the smoke from the fire ended and the
dust began. A small ceaseless wind kept it in motion
and drew an occasional faint chime from the bell.
The two men by the fire were speaking in low tones,
as though the dust had muted their voices.

"The Duchess of Borges spoke truly, God rest her

soul, when she called this the loneliest place in the world."

"That's Brother Gregory, the hedgehog," whispered Fox. "Isn't he sweet?"

The name hedgehog suited him. He had just such a little wedge-shaped face as a hedgehog, I thought.

"More truly than she knew," said the other man, a tall, thin, angular person with a dark sorrowful face. He stood up now and loomed over the fire. "Heaven defend us from the legacies of pious ladies. I could wish that her relatives might have profited from her will. The cost of endowing this mission would have bought sufficient masses to release her from Purgatory and we could have been left in exemplary poverty in Spain and nobody the worse. The Duchess of Borges's generosity to the church has no doubt spelled damnation to several chuchmen."

"A deathbed folly," sighed the little man. "Old ladies are frequently whimsical. But the flock, Brother, the flock. Have they struggled against the faith? Have you not subdued the heathen and brought them to the fold?"

The tall priest laughed. "Oh, they have come to the fold. They have surrendered the jaguar for the cross and scarcely marked the difference. To all my exhortations they have responded with a simple 'Yes,

Father. So be it, Father.' They celebrate the feasts and the saints' days with the docility of the first Christians. I had hoped for martyrdom — and found it. I have had no one to talk to for three years."

"How have you lived, Brother?" asked Brother Gregory.

"On two letters a year from the Mother House in Mexico. The Archbishop has been pleased to commend my patience. One letter came from the Cardinal José Maria de Santa Eulalia, also commending my efforts. That child must be rising sixteen by now."

"Nearer seventeen," replied Brother Gregory. "They say he drinks and gambles."

"His Eminence was pleased to offer me his congratulations on my vocation and to commend me for spreading the gospel in this remote corner of the Indies, establishing the cornerstone of that great edifice from whence a royal road will run to the furthest reaches of El Dorado, to the Straits of Anian themselves. It was a splendid letter. Whoever wrote it was a scholar and a diplomat. Speaking of the Straits, has there been word of their discovery?"

"No word," replied Brother Gregory. "They say they lie well to the north of Mexico and further west. Do your Indians not tell of them?"

"They have never heard of them. Their world is

bounded by the edges of this plain. They know nothing of the ocean. The mysteries of the Christian religion appear to them simple and easily grasped. They say their prayers and continue with the business of getting enough food to stay alive. But if confronted with a great body of water they could not comprehend it.

"A sea bird blew in here once. It was nearly dead and died quickly. I marked the species. My people were inclined to pray to it, but when it died they saw that it was no more than a bird. No more than a bird! It is the birds which have kept me alive, Brother Gregory. You will scarcely believe what I have done for God. I have described every bird which has come here, native and foreign. No man on earth knows more of the birds of this country than I do. My Christians are my cross and the birds are my crown. For all I know, they are hatched on the shores of the great Straits. It is hard to believe that this desolation could bloom with birds, unless they were vultures, which we have in good supply. They are harmless, ugly things, and no doubt do their share of God's work. But the others, the great orange bird and the blue bird like a piece of burning sky, both pass over this plain. Eagles sweep the sky on their way westward. I watch them all. I could tell you every individual that passes.

"Surely these are signs that the great Straits are not so distant. And if the jaguar is here, what may we expect from the Straits themselves? The phoenix? The unicorn? The lion and the camelopard? Even Behemoth himself, who served Hannibal in battle! My prayers will have been answered when I have set eyes on these. God has intended me to see these things or I should not be here."

"My prayers have been more easily answered," said the tall man. "I prayed that they would send me someone to talk to and they have. You. It is only just that you should be vouchsafed your unicorn."

"You shall build the royal road, Brother Martin," said Gregory, "to the Straits of Anian. And I shall fill the world with portraits of the beasts of God. God did not intend us to remain here. The task is done here. The Indians are Christians. They cannot be made more so than they are already. We shall perhaps find less biddable savages on the shores of the Straits — thus the work is more ennobled — and we shall find the great beasts."

Out of the shadows Guelph gave a long whinny of mirth. Brother Martin peered in our direction.

"My wits must be wandering. I could have sworn that I heard a horse."

"What will they say when they see Guelph?" whispered Caspar. "After all that talk about beasts."

"They won't believe it," said Fox. "They'll just go on thinking it's all the disordered vision of an unhinged mind. That's what Brother Martin said when he first saw me. He believed in Gregory but he thought I was something you see when you eat mushrooms. Except he hasn't eaten any mushrooms. But now he's forgotten about me and he thinks Brother Gregory got sent in the ordinary way because he wrote home and asked for him. He thinks your cardinal sent him."

"He got more than he bargained for," I muttered. "The cardinal's here. And don't call him mine. He's just as much yours, if it comes to that."

"What does Brother Gregory make of it all?" inquired Caspar.

"It all happened so fast I don't think he had time to think anything. You remember how it was when we got into the garden. There was a change of light."

"He never thinks anyway," interposed Guapo, who was squirming in Fox's arms. "And he won't care whether it's a dream or not, as long as he can see the birds and the animals and paint them. He wants to get to the Straits of Anian because of all the wonderful wild life. Most Spaniards are after the gold. There is no gold in the Straits, as Guelph can tell you, but there *are* unicorns."

"Guapo," said José, "I am astounded to see you, Guapo."

"Good evening, Eminence. Love and duty to you."

"Ah," said José, "so you can talk too. I might have known."

"Of course I can talk," replied the dog. "But it didn't seem politic to talk to you."

"How did you leave my cousin Margarita?"

"As usual," answered Guapo. "She was putting your uncle, the Inquisitor, out of countenance. He's a worthy man, but he has no sense of humor. You yourself were causing dissension among the troops about a stray horse which you claimed was a unicorn. It was regarded as just another instance of Your Lordship's incurable flightiness. There's some question as to whether the decision to make Your Lordship a cardinal, especially at so early an age, was a wise one."

"If we find the Straits," said José meditatively, "they will find the question beside the point. All power will be mine. I shall be the greatest of the

Conquistadores — the Hapsburg of Hapsburgs, the discoverer of the undiscoverable."

"But there is no gold, Eminence," whispered Balthasar.

"I must have gold," said the cardinal.

"But never from Anian."

As though he had overheard the conversation, Brother Gregory was pursuing the subject of the Straits. "Tell me what you know of Anian, Brother," he begged.

"Our explorers have been searching for Anian for a hundred years," replied Brother Martin. "We are told that the Straits swarm with the most delicate and nourishing fish and that the seabirds bring up from their depths pearls as big as robins' eggs.

"The great Commander Hernando de Cortez believed he would find them in this vicinity. He found the pyramid of the sun where Quetzlcoatl prophesied the coming of strange gods on great four-footed beasts. He saw the flower city of Xochimilco, with its canals winding like the serpent of Eden amongst the golden poplars. He saw blood streaming from the altars of Huizilopochtli and added his own tributary to that terrible river but he never found the treasure of the Aztecs. For all I know they may have sunk it in the Straits. They heaved up mountains over their ziggurats and clenched their teeth in Cortez's fires, biting back the secret when the flames consumed their flesh. Cortez saw much blood but little wealth. When he sailed in search of Anian, the tides drew him on but he never reached their waters. All my life I have hungered for them, but I know that I shall never see them. I have lodged my spirit with the birds of this peninsula. They are my Anian."

"Have we not been taught, Brother, to perceive God's purpose in God's signs?" said Brother Gregory. "If we were not intended to find the Straits we should not be seeking them. The Indians do not need us. It is the Straits which call us."

"Then," cried José out of the shadows, "we go together in the name of God and the King of Spain." He rode Balthasar into the ring of light shed by the fire and stood up tall in his stirrups. He was magnificent. "We shall conquer the Straits as we conquered the Indies."

The two priests looked up slowly from the fire. I should have thought they would have been stunned by fear or astonishment or both, but they appeared to take the visitation as part of the grand design or whatever they call it. José on his white horse shone crimson above them in the firelight. Brother Martin broke into a smile. "The dream goes on," he said.

"I am not a dream," said José insistently. "I am your prince. You may kiss my ring." He held out his hand and the cardinal's ring glittered on his finger.

The two Brothers rose to their feet and came forward.

"Your Eminence appears wonderfully substantial," said Brother Martin. "Even as a dream Your Eminence is profoundly welcome. My prayers have been indeed answered. I have been made mad, but the madness is good. I kiss the ring."

He bowed ceremoniously over the outstretched hand and drew back. Brother Gregory scuttled forward, bobbed over the white hand and its jewel, and squinted up into José's face.

"His very face and shape," he whispered. "He is better than a painting of himself. I wonder if he has the dice. I shall believe him when he shakes his double sixes."

"Only a generation of vipers requires a sign," said José sternly. "But since it is a sign that you wish, here are your dice." He took the dice from his trouser pocket and dropped them in the dust.

"You will know him by the dice," said Gregory. "It is he."

"Gregory, you have lived with your pictures too

long and cannot tell dreams from nature. This cardinal is a dream."

"Dreams and cardinals are a part of nature, Brother," said Gregory.

"Good friars, will you dispute the evidence of your senses?" said José. "I am no mad monk's dream but your cardinal brought here by the unicorn to find the sacred treasure of the Aztecs. It is I who shall lead you to the gold that lies on the shores of the Straits — "

"And to the unicorn?" cried Brother Gregory. "If Your Eminence will lead us to the unicorn, I shall believe in you if Your Eminence were twenty times a dream."

"There is no treasure," said Brother Martin, "and for all we know, the Straits themselves are a dream. They are not to be conquered."

"The treasure exists," said José. "I have a part of it here." He drew forth the quetzl and held it up to the firelight. "It is mine. I have claimed it for my cousin, the young infanta. It fell into my hands and I accepted it as a sign that it was destined for me and the glory of my line."

"Your Eminence stole the bird?" asked Brother Martin.

"I am incapable of theft. I claimed it."

"You must understand how deficient in moral understanding the Indians are," said Brother Martin. "My flock would assume that Your Lordship had stolen the bird, a piece of impertinence for which they must be pardoned on grounds of invincible ignorance. The Indians would not think the worse of Your Lordship for having taken possession of the idol. Such an act would merely serve to show that Your Lordship shared a common humanity with them. But they would dread the inevitable consequences of removing the quetzl from its native climes. Your Lordship does not intend to take it from Mexico, I trust."

"Why should I not? I owe it to the family."

"It is sacred and might do much harm to the innocent."

"May I remind you, Brother, that the bird is a heathen idol of immense value but without power. Observe the stones with which it is encrusted. It is worth a prince's ransom. It is an object of worship to unbelievers so it can surely do devout Christians no harm. We would be impervious to it."

"Your Lordship's reasoning would confound Aristotle," said Brother Martin courteously. "But all the same I entreat Your Lordship to leave the bird on Indian soil. Their birds are of fire and air and not for us. Their gods are bloody as Moloch and more furious than Lucifer. Leave the bird, Your Eminence."

"Brother," said José sardonically, "have you fallen prey to their folly yourself? You seem to think that the bird is holy. It is nothing but booty."

Guelph gave a threatening whinny.

"How your horse cries out," said Brother Martin. "The jaguar must be near."

"What is the jaguar?" asked José.

"The jaguar god. Where the bird goes the jaguar goes too. You are warned, Eminence."

"I have dominion over the bird," said José carelessly. "I can show you marvels against which no idol in Christendom can lift claw or feather. I have come here by the power of the unicorn and the bird is my spoil. I am not afraid of it. I am not afraid of anything."

"He's singing a different tune, isn't he," whispered Caspar. "He was scared enough this morning."

"He's adjusted," I answered. "I knew he would, but he's adjusted too much."

"Far too much," agreed Guelph. "He's a foolish boy and comes of a foolish family. He will keep the bird. There is no use in warning him. An empire will fall and emperors will rot in its ruins and the quetzl will fly home."

"I shall keep the quetzl." José spoke angrily now. It did not suit him to be crossed. "I shall toss it into the Straits rather than leave it here."

"The Straits keep nothing foreign to them," said Guelph gently. "You can be sure the Straits will never hold the quetzl."

"I beseech Your Lordship to leave us, if that is Your Lordship's determination," Brother Martin was saying. "If the unicorn brought Your Lordship here, he may equally take you hence."

"Before he goes," said Gregory, "I hope he will let us gaze upon the unicorn."

"That should be no trouble at all," said Fox, breaking in with determination. "And it isn't up to the cardinal. The unicorn is right here, Brother Hedgehog. Just speak to him and he'll show himself. I know he will."

Her voice came shrill through the dusty air. It startled both the brothers more than the vision of José on his horse or even the quetzl in his hand. "Come here, Guelph, and let Brother Gregory see you. That's why we came here, after all."

Brother Martin had taken a step across the space that lay between us and the fire, and came short up against Guelph's white muzzle and glittering horn. Fox was standing beside him with Guapo in her arms.

"It's really all right, Brother Martin," she said. "I daresay you think you're still dreaming but if you are, then we all are."

Brother Martin looked down at her with a stern, puzzled expression on his face. I suppose he was one of those people who never makes a noise about things.

"Little ghost," he said, and smiled. "Well, I knew a gypsy once who prophesied half a century ago in Madrid that I should meet a strange fate in a strange land. You are enough like her to be her grand-daughter. She half promised me the Straits of Anian then. Have you come to show them to me?"

"I expect so. We seem to bring people things they would like to see. Like bringing Brother Gregory together with the unicorn. Look, Brother Hedgehog, now you can paint a picture of him exactly as he is."

Brother Gregory was staring at Guelph open-mouthed.

"His feet are not as we have been told," he said. "The unicorn has the feet of Behemoth. His horn is a potent weapon of Cupid — "

"There is no instance in which it has been used for that or any other purpose not my own," said Guelph calmly, although his eyes were perilously bright with anger. "As for my feet, anything less like an elephant's — " He pawed the dust with one delicate hoof, its edge sharp as a razor. Guelph continued, turning to us: "Men talk of magic as though it would serve their turns and obey their rulings. Brother Gregory believes that I have an elephant's hooves because he painted them on me. My lord cardinal believes that the Straits of Anian are full of gold for the convenience of Spaniards. You all can see the very Straits and move through their magic but they lie beyond your imaginations, west of all your dreams. We shall go to the Straits because the words of power have been said and they cannot be unsaid. Who goes with us now? Whether we go over the glass mountain or through the mole's tunnel, we shall go to the Straits."

"Shall we see the heraldic beasts?" asked Gregory. "Shall I fill my canvases with their portraits?"

"Shall I claim them for the family?" asked José.

"I don't see how anyone can expect me to go over a glass mountain," said Black Beauty. "I haven't the feet for it."

"Perhaps you can go through the tunnel instead," said Caspar consolingly.

"I must go to Anian," said Guapo. "I've never caught a rabbit. Perhaps I shall catch one there."

"I cannot leave the birds," said Brother Martin.

"Go to the Straits, Gregory. I have had my evening's conversation. And I chose my road years ago. All others lead away from here."

"But shall we ever get home again?" asked Fox anxiously.

"The third road is there in the thicket," I said. "It leads to the meadows. We are never far from home."

"Oh dear," cried Fox. "I can't make up my mind. I wish I were at the Straits. I wish I were home doing something safe and boring. Like making sand castles. I'm afraid of dreaming. Let us get away from the dream."

"At the edge of the sea," said Balthasar. "O Thalassa."

❖❖❖ EIGHT ❖❖❖❖❖

THE MIST was rising as it usually does about the middle of each day. I could see the whole outline of the promontory. It is called, as every sane person knows — that is what my grandfather says when he tells you something that no sane person knows — Point Lobos. Wolf Point in English, but the place is shaped like a lion, a sphinx couchant.

We seemed to have been building our castle for hours on the lonely beach. High up on the dunes a man in a brown poncho was sketching. And a little dog watched us from a dry spot well above the tide line. He had frisked along at our heels after we had left the carnival and now seemed to adopt us. I suppose we are the sort of people who are liked by dogs.

134

"Did you like playing with the Hapgood girl?" I asked Fox.

"She's too old for me," said Fox, "and rather silly. She's rehearsing in the play and to hear her talk you'd think she was Sophia Loren. Where's that boy you were with? He looked rather nasty to me."

"He got in a fight," I answered, "and he couldn't talk about anything but his family. He thinks he's somebody. He's sort of a tourist — or a hippie. I don't think he's ever been here before."

"What makes you say he's a hippie?" asked Fox.

"Oh, his hair was long, and he wasn't very clean. And now I come to think of it, he had a fancy sort of ring."

"Was he all by himself?"

"I expect so. Or perhaps he wasn't. Hippies usually go in herds, don't they?"

"That's partridges," said Caspar. "Or maybe it's deer." He took some wet sand in his fingers and began to dribble it on a tower of our castle. The castle consisted of four main towers connected by channels over which we had thrown bridges leading to the main gates. The walls of the towers were buttressed with mussel shells and the bridges were made of driftwood. I had found a little abalone shell and set

it in the gate facing the sea, making a hatchment of pearl.

The beaches here below Point Lobos are covered with fine white sand like powder, and in the coves and inlets you can find all manner of shells and pebbles. We studded the castle with conches and scallop shells, mussels and periwinkles. We set sea urchins to guard the gates and the castle was beginning to look like the Kremlin.

Once you start building a really important sand castle it is hard to leave it to the tide. We built it high and firm so, when the sea should come, it would not injure the main walls. I dug with both my hands and feet to make the channel as deep as possible, and Fox and Caspar dragged up seaweed, both the wide ribbony kind and the green lettucey kind, to hang like garlands over the gateways. The dog, a little spaniel, came down from the warm dunes and helped us dig.

"He's a lovely dog," said Fox. "I wish he were ours."

The dog barked loudly at this and Caspar said, "He thinks he is."

"Oh, he's somebody's pet," said Fox. "Look how well kept he is. Perhaps he belongs to that man who's sketching."

Perhaps he did or perhaps he didn't. Anyway, he stuck to us all afternoon, digging in the sand, running up and down the beach and answering the seals who called incessantly from the rock.

It was one of those queer afternoons when everything seems a little out of focus. I felt that we were somewhere between things as they really are and the way they seem. The morning had been so foggy and now the afternoon was so clear that it made you wonder if you lived in one world or two.

I wanted badly to find a really enormous abalone

but the big ones don't wash up on the beaches very often. They are too special, I guess. I have always hoped that if I looked at one long enough I might really see colors that nobody had ever seen before. I wanted to go up to the Point and have a look for one, but Fox thought that was a stupid idea.

"You might get caught by the abalone and then the tide would come along and drown you."

"I won't try to take one that's fixed to a rock," I said. "I'll just find a loose one. Come on, Caspar."

Fox said that would be better but Caspar said he wouldn't go shell-hunting until he had eaten something. "It's been centuries since breakfast," he said. "I feel as though I hadn't eaten since I was born." Once he began to talk about food I found myself assailed by the pangs of hunger too, and so we agreed to go home and find some lunch.

We climbed the dunes, passing close by the man who was sketching. It was Brother Gregory from the Mission.

He peered at us with bright little eyes as we approached him. We waved to him and he flicked a little clawlike hand at us.

The kitchen clock said three when we slipped in the back door. There is something flat about three o'clock. It is not really time for anything. If you are little you have just waked up from a nap and you are cross. If you are bigger, as we are, it is time to think about what to do next. We took some bread and cheese and fruit into the orchard, sat down under a grapefruit tree, and considered.

"I wonder what the play is," said Fox. "She's never told us what it's about. How mysterious she is! Anyone else would have given us the whole story and what part she's playing and whether or not she's the star."

I agreed that most grown-ups have a way of letting you know indirectly what they are up to. With our grandmother, however, every move is a surprise. She was like an extra queen on the chessboard.

"I'd like to see her act," I said. I couldn't imagine what part she would take. It was hard to imagine her as anything outside of herself. She would wear a part as she wore clothes — as she had worn for a moment the red robe of the cardinal taken from the chest in the drawing room. She was one of those people who leave a stain on the air where they have passed. I could feel her presence in the golden gloom of the grapefruit tree and in the scent of oranges and lemons.

These thoughts filtered through my mind as I

munched contentedly at a piece of cheese. Caspar, lying on his back, ate an alligator pear.

"Hey, that's my alligator," said Fox.

"That's all right," said Caspar amiably. "You can have it back. I haven't swallowed it yet."

She gave a snort of disgust. "You really are the most ridiculous child."

"No more ridiculous than you. It's ridiculous to be a girl."

That is the sort of conversation you have at three o'clock in the afternoon.

When we got back to the beach the tide was going out. The water stood glassy in the moat and the sun glanced off the shells and pebbles. We stood on the dune, gazing at our creation with love and admiration. It was a castle whose walls clearly held magnificent secrets. I heard a short, sharp bark and the little spaniel came frisking up with sand in his feathers.

"He keeps popping up, doesn't he," said Fox. "I wish I'd brought him something to eat. Here doggie, nice doggie."

The sight of the dog gave me a good deal of pleasure, as though I were seeing an old friend. Dogs often give you that impression, but with this dog the feeling was so strong that I thought I must have known him elsewhere. There was something emphatic about this dog. He was sending signals.

"He wants to show us something," said Fox. "Isn't he cute? What's on your mind, fellow?"

Whatever was on his mind seemed to take him in the direction of the Mission. He frisked off toward it, stopping every now and then to see if we were following him. We decided to humor him. Besides we were curious. I wondered if he were earning himself a life-saving medal. Perhaps the Mission was burning or burglars were holding the congregation at bay while they stole its treasures.

But the Mission was not burning. It crouched in its hollow soaking up the pale sunlight. The wind blew sharply from the sea and I shivered as we came into the garden. It had been summer down on the dunes but it was winter here in this hollow. I noticed that the vines were green around the Mission as though there had been recent rain.

There was a good deal of activity in the courtyard. An old monk sat cross-legged by the fountain, surrounded by a group of children who chattered like birds. They were dressed in bright colors — turkey reds, cobalt blues, sharp greens, and flamboyant pinks and yellows — and wore feathers in their hair. Some children were writing on slates, other were chanting lessons, but most of them were at games, tossing balls, playing leapfrog.

"They must be the Saint Filomena children," said Caspar. "The ones the carnival is in aid of."

"They look like Indians," said Fox.

The dog ran into the midst of the crowd barking, then stopped and looked over his shoulder at us, as though asking us to come nearer. We obeyed, making our way among the children.

As we approached the fountain we saw that the old man was sewing. Brightly colored piles of children's clothing lay in heaps around him, and as he finished one garment he would toss it onto a pile and choose another to work on. Sometimes a child would skip to the pile, choose out something that took his fancy, and flutter off with it.

"Imagine that," whispered Fox. "He's a dress-maker. What an odd thing for a monk to do!"

"Amar a Dios," said a voice, "who else is to clothe them?"

The voice belonged to a dark somber-faced youth, standing near to the fountain. He was a little older than most of the children and was wearing a brown tunic, hitched above the knees but cowled like a monk's robe.

"I only meant," said Fox, "that you don't often see monks sewing."

"Fray Juniperro Serra is a master of every craft. How would the women learn to sew if he did not teach them? Friars don't travel with seamstresses."

"He makes very pretty clothes," said Fox.

"Our Indians like their adornments to be handsome."

"I didn't know there would be Indians here," I said.

The boy gave me an odd look. "Whom did you expect to find?" he asked.

"Well, not anyone exactly," I answered. "We were just out for a walk."

The boy looked puzzled. "But you are Spanish children? You must have come from the ship."

"No ship," said Caspar. "We came from the beach and we aren't Spanish."

"You can scarcely expect me to believe that you are Indians," said the boy, "and if you did not come from the ship, where could you have come from? We have been waiting for the ship. It is to bring the bells from Mexico City."

"We don't know anything about the bells," said Caspar. "Who sent for them?"

"Father Serra, of course. He loves those cast in Mexico even better than the Spanish ones. Nine missions have risen at his bidding from Alcalá to Yerba Buena, but to him a mission without a bell is a thought without speech. When you came over the hill I thought you must bring news of the bells."

"No," I said. "I'm very sorry. If we had known —" I tried to sort out what was happening. "We were building sand castles — that is, *a* sand castle. Brother Gregory was sketching. And then the dog came and brought us here. I don't know why. Did he think we had the bells?"

"Ah, Guapo," said the boy and snapped his fingers. The dog came dancing up to him.

"He wanted to show us the Mission, I guess," said Caspar. "He's been running around our castle all afternoon. He's a lovely dog. Is he yours?"

"No. He belongs to the Mission. Guapo was brought out from Spain. He and I came together. It is lonely here and a faithful dog can be a great solace. The Indians understand these things. When I first came I suffered greatly from solitude. They brought me a basket of kittens."

"That was thoughtful of them," said Fox.

"They are naturally charitable," said the boy. "They believed the kittens would cure me."

"And did they?" asked Fox.

"Yes," said the boy. "They put the kittens in my bed and that cured me. I took them as a sign from the founder of our order, the blessed Saint Francis. It was the loneliness of which I sickened. The Indians know that animals cure loneliness. They are a good cure although not the only one. Brother Gregory, now — he writes plays and paints pictures."

"Oh yes," said Fox. "We know about that. He's working on a play now."

"Yes," said the boy. *"Lucifer and Gabriel.* Our people love to act. He has written them very long speeches to declaim. A spendid argument. But how did you know about the play?"

"Everyone's been talking about it," said Caspar. "You weren't expecting to keep it a secret, were you?"

"No. But beyond the Mission walls there is nobody to tell of it."

"I wish we could stop to see it," said Fox, "but I don't know if we'll be allowed. Especially as we're going to the other play tomorrow night."

"There is no other play," said the boy flatly. "There is only Gregory's Christmas play. It is for this that we want the bells — to ring in the Nativity after the defeat of Lucifer."

"Christmas!" I exclaimed. "But this isn't Christmas. It's the middle of July."

The wind whistled in the leaves of the olive trees and the old father coughed and drew his cowl around his neck. The boy seemed not to have heard what I said. He stepped over to Father Serra and said, "It grows chilly, Father. Won't you go in?"

The old father looked up and saw us for the first time.

"Spanish children!" he exclaimed. "Then the ship must have arrived and the bells are here."

I opened my mouth to speak when the dog barked sharply and said, "Don't disappoint him."

"Guapo," I said. "It's you!"

"Of course it's me," said Guapo. "Who did you suppose it was? You've been wool-gathering. I thought you'd never wake up."

"But where are we?"

"In the gardens of San Carlos Borromeo. The Cathedral Mission."

"I know that," I said. "I mean when?"

"It's 1776, I think," said Guapo, "but I've never been too good at dates. There's a play being done. The Indians love to act and Father Serra and the brothers love to see a play. It's a pity about the bells. Everyone was counting on them, especially the children. They would have been so effective. A grand peal when Gabriel finally refutes Lucifer and casts him down and then everyone, even the Mission animals, come up to the manger at the High Altar. I was planning to take part in the procession myself. It really is a great disappointment to do without the bells. The children have been so looking forward to hearing them."

"Oh," cried Fox. "But they must have bells. What about Guelph? Surely he could do something about them."

"There, I knew you'd think of something," said Guapo. "That was why I brought you. I'd have called Guelph myself but, to be frank, I've always had a bit of difficulty with the words of power. But you pronounce them wonderfully and, since we are at the very gates of Hy Breasil, perhaps Guelph would oblige with a little extra effort. And think what it would mean to Gregory and to José."

"José?" I asked. "Is he here?"

"Don't you recognize him?" asked Guapo.

"You mean — that boy?"

"A century or so does make a difference, doesn't it," said Guapo. "He followed Brother Gregory to the Straits and found himself here. He stole the bird, you know. And the Straits of Anian wouldn't have him. He learned quite a lesson."

"He doesn't seem to know who he is," said Caspar.

"He will," said Guapo. "Just as you did."

Fox crossed over to where Father Serra sat sewing. Every now and then he coughed slightly. He looked up at her, bright-eyed and sweet-faced.

"Good evening, Father," said Fox.

"Amar a Dios, child," said Father Serra. "What can I do for you? Would you like a new frock?"

"Would you like a new bell?" asked Fox.

Father Serra looked up from his sewing. "The ships have not come," he said gently. "We must be patient. It is a disappointment, but it cannot be helped."

A number of the Indian children had approached Fox curiously and were listening to her with interest. She turned from the father to the child nearest her, a girl dressed in scarlet with turquoises in her ears, and said, "Do you want the bells for Christmas?"

The girl nodded and said, "Yes. We've been waiting a long time."

Several other children nodded their heads in agreement. "Yes, we've been waiting. We thought surely they would come for Christmas Eve."

"Guelph!" cried Fox. "Bring us the bells for

Father Serra's Christmas play. Come, Guelph. Come, sweet Guelph." She turned to the group of children. "Say after me!" she said. "Say very clearly what I say." And she gave the words of power. In a high lilting chorus the Indian children chanted after her; over and over again they said the words. They made a sound like the sea, a sound like hawks crying across the sky, and then a sound like a great carillon.

I looked up into the bell tower and saw the sun glinting on the bronze flanks of three noble bells calling Christmas from the domed belfry of San Carlos Borromeo.

And in the Mission pasture, the familiar pasture which we passed on the way to and from the station, three horses were grazing and one had a horn between the eyes.

"José," I said, "The horses have come. And we are at the Gates of Hy Breasil. Are you coming with us? This must be the end of the journey that we've been looking for."

# NINE

O they rade on, and farther on,
And they waded rivers abune the knee;
And they saw neither sun nor moon,
But they heard the roaring of the sea.

IT WAS PART of the ballad which our grandfather had quoted and it kept running through my head in time with the horses' hooves. We twisted and turned through a watery twilight which edged everything with gold. The air was full of sounds. Sometimes I thought I heard birds singing and sometimes their voices mingled and were lost among the notes of distant horns and the chiming of bells. When I looked down I was not sure that there was any ground to touch. I seemed to be swimming in air.

"Where is the path?" I said, peering through the shining dusk. "I can't see it."

"You can't see it because you're part of it," said Guelph. Fox and I were riding him, and Guapo was running alongside.

"We're in the Straits. They surround Hy Breasil."

"But where *is* Hy Breasil?"

"You should know. You made it."

"I didn't know I was making it."

"You and many others. Brother Hedgehog makes it, the gypsy queen makes it. You made it at the edge of the sea. You're making it now. Don't you remember?"

Through the mist I could see our beach and the castle rising at the edge of the sea. It appeared a great distance away, a tiny castle against a silky blue sea, with people moving about it. Fox was there; the copper lights in her hair gleamed in the sun and a glow of sunburn showed on Caspar's shoulders.

"He should put on his T-shirt," I said. "He always gets a bad burn."

Guelph gave a little neigh of amusement. "He'll notice presently, and if he doesn't, Fox will."

I could see myself on the other side of the castle, stooping down to pick something from the sand. It was an abalone shell. I saw the shimmering hollow in the hand of my other self. Silvery pink and peacock blue and queer rays of yellow melted into whirls of green and purple.

"I've found a shell," I cried. "Just the very one I wanted."

Fox, coming up behind me, cried, "Oh, what a beauty!"

It was the light from the shell which shone around us. It must have been, because when I looked up I could see no sun nor was there a moon. Too soft for the sun and too bright for the moon, the light must have come from the shell arching over us like a dome, lighting us on our way.

Balthasar, the sea horse, was gliding alongside me, his treble clef tail fanning the warm golden air and leaving behind him a filmy wake. His rider was the cardinal. One thing I must allow our cardinal — he sat a horse better than any television cowboy. In the cardinal's hands Balthasar was made of white coral and foam; he moved in time to the tides. The cardinal's red cloak streamed behind him and on one imperial wrist there perched a bird. Bird, horseman, and horse gazed ahead, as I did, seeing all their centuries. The bird fluttered from his wrist and spread itself like a huge eagle over the palace gardens. The wings stretched from east to west until they covered the kingdom in shadow. Beneath the wings children played with their attendants, their dwarfs, their pets. Sleek mastiffs paced at the heels of a melancholy king, a painted queen moved stiffly from garden to palace to curtained bedchamber to royal tomb. With grave eyes, the cardinal observed the pageant of his memory. Somewhere a fountain splashed, throwing jets of water in the air. Everything smelled of oranges. He saw himself, bored in the hot, still sunlight, looking about for something to tease: a girl, an animal, someone who couldn't tease back. Tormenting dwarfs gave the cardinal no pleasure; they had to put up with it and he felt nothing but contempt for them. The girl, his cousin, was dangerous to tease. She turned from him in high displeasure when he snatched a fig from her and popped it into his own mouth. He should have known better — an animal who displeased her might be beaten, a dwarf could be sent back to the charcoal burners who had raised him. Even a cardinal could be returned to the Jesuit fathers who had caned him into etiquette and Latin and would not be happy to see him back.

His cousin stood surrounded by her enormous skirt, the guard-infanta. Deviling her required the tactics of raising siege to a citadel. He loved her because she was little, beautiful, noble, and had the best of him.

"I shall be Empress of Austria and then you will do everything I say and if you do not, I shall have you flogged."

"I shall do everything Your Imperial Highness asks. But you shall see. I shall become a conquistador. I shall go to Mexico and kill Indians and find the treasure."

"The Indies belong to me. I shall send you to the dungeons if you steal my treasure."

"I'll play you for the Indies. I shall wager one of my hawks against your Indies."

"I don't want your silly hawks. What should I do with such a bird? Such claws and such a beak! Thank you, Cousin, but I shall keep the Indies."

But the cardinal had thrown the dice. A pair of sixes chattered on the terrace like teeth.

"I've won, Your Highness. I shall have the Indies and you will have my bird."

"But I never laid a wager," complained the princess. "And I don't want a bird. Not any bird at all."

"I shall give you the treasure of the Aztecs. It is a bird, solid gold through and through and studded with diamonds and emeralds. I shall give it to you for a wedding gift."

"What would I want with such a bird? It can't even sing."

"Nevertheless, you shall have it."

"No, I tell you. No."

"You can't escape it. I stole it especially for you."

"It is a cruel bird. I hate it."

The dice rattled again on the flagstones. The bird flew to a soldier in armor, to a courtier in black velvet, to a bride, to a widow, to another bride, and back to a soldier in a scarlet uniform. The soldier stood like a king and light flickered in his red hair and tawny beard. Drums rattled around him and the shadow of the bird darkened the landscape. It flew back to the Indian from whom it had been snatched. The Indian bent and kissed the jeweled head.

"The Indies are lost," whispered Guelph. "The bird flew home to Montezuma at last. Your cousin Maximilian is dead. Your Eminence should never have brought Quetzlcoatl away. He carried nothing but grief."

"But that was after my time," said José. "How was I to know?"

"You might have taken warning."

"But I did it all for the family and the glory of God. And the guns are silent now."

"They are never silent," said Guelph. "And in the end you will play the part of the Indian."

We could hear the guns quite clearly, under bird-song and over bell-sound. I saw José put his hands to his ears. "I shall remember no more," he cried. "I shall run away. Let the Indies go. I have nothing to do with them. You brought me here and so I have escaped. I am in the Straits of Anian. Hy Breasil is at hand."

"But you can't escape there." It was the voice of Balthasar, rising like a wave as he cantered. "You can come to it but you can't stay in it. It is no escape. The winds are colder here than at the Poles. The fires of Popocatepetl are faint in comparison to the flames of Hy Breasil. You can touch its searing sands and its savage flowers but you can never live with them. Your Eminence has tried to escape too often. Elfland is no haven."

There was a sturdy clip-clop of hooves. Caspar on Black Beauty came trotting alongside, peering through the golden shadows.

"I think it's fun," he said. "Why do you make it sound like some kind of doom, Guelph?"

"It is a doom," said Guelph. "It is the gold and crimson doom of emperors, the brazen doom of soldiers, and the green and bloody doom of hunters."

"Well, it's my doom too," said Caspar. "And Black Beauty's. There are wonderful things up ahead. I can see all the things I remember and a lot of others that I would like to remember. I wonder what Brother Gregory remembers."

"He isn't looking back," said Guelph. "The Straits of Anian are his goal. He has work to do there. The beasts are waiting for him."

As Guelph spoke the hedgehog priest appeared ahead of us, his brown robes floating about him. Gryphons with green, shining scales stood over him like sentries. Winged lions and singing dolphins romped around him. He stopped continually to talk to them. They croaked and clanged to him, flapped their bat wings and rolled their crimson eyeballs. They found him funny. Guelph tossed up his head and gave an amused whinny.

"He should afford Madam Sphinx enough entertainment to last her for centuries," said the unicorn. "He will think of her shortly."

And he did. I could see him do it. She took form in the shining mist — great cat body and mysterious human head high above the heroic talons. Gregory frisked up to her quick as a squirrel and stopped between the terrible paws.

"Ah, Madam," he cried. "How long, how long!

We meet at last. What a time it has been! Ever since I can remember."

The sphinx shifted position slightly and looked down at the artist. Then she burst out laughing. I wish I could describe the laughter of the sphinx. It isn't like any sound I ever heard on earth. But then, of course, I suppose we weren't on earth. The sphinx only laughs in Hy Breasil.

"Well, Hedgehog," she said. "I hope you are not disappointed. You've worked hard enough for this meeting."

He stood back and looked at her as he had looked at Guelph. "I can't say, Madam, that you are exactly as I have pictured you. You are greater and more golden. In my memory you were darker — and smaller — more human, somehow. But memory deceives, does it not! I was deceived in Guelph, the unicorn too. I fancied that he would have elephant's feet. Well, well, I see I must paint your portrait again."

From behind me I heard Caspar's voice. "I've seen her before somewhere," he said.

"Very likely." It was Guapo. "She was there when I was visiting the palace of Rameses II with Guelph. Handsome, isn't she!"

"Is that you, Guapo?" said the sphinx. "How does it go with you?"

"Well, thank you, Ladyship. And I hope you keep well."

"I can't complain," said the sphinx. "They miss you at court. You have become a minor deity and your sarcophagus made the designer's name famous all over Egypt. He's done very well in the cat and dog line since. His Anubis is the talk of Memphis."

"I'm honored, I'm sure," said Guapo. "Egypt was an enriching experience, although I've given my heart to Spain. In the end I'm a one princess dog."

"Ah," said the sphinx, "the point is to find the princess. Well, you are very fortunate, Guapo. And Guelph, you are welcome as always. What brings you to the Straits this time?"

"May it please Your Ladyship," said Guelph, cantering smoothly forward to the feet of the sphinx, "the words of power were uttered. I answered the summons and it brought me to a pasture above the western seas where I encountered three children. But as Your Ladyship is aware, the ways of the words of power are likely to lead to inscrutable ends."

"You have the children with you, and a fourth besides. Aren't they afraid, Guelph?"

"A grandee of Spain fears nothing," exclaimed José indignantly.

I didn't know what the penalties for telling tales in Hy Breasil were, but if José was going in for lies I thought I might as well, too.

"Of course we aren't afraid," I said.

Huge agate eyes gazed down at me, the pupils only partly in eclipse in the golden dusk. I had to own to myself that I was very much afraid — more afraid than I had been at any time in our adventure. José was pale with fear. It was a special kind of fear, different from the kind of scare he had taken over the light switch. It was the kind of fear that you feel when you know for the first time that there is something so much bigger than you that perhaps you don't count very much at all. I could see that both Fox and Caspar shared our fear, but when I looked at Gregory I knew that he didn't. He had taken out his painting things. He took them from a knapsack slung over his shoulder and was preparing to make a picture of the sphinx. The difference between Gregory and the rest of us was clear. He didn't know that he existed — or, if he did, he didn't care. The only thing that mattered to him were the things he painted. They were his existence.

"If Madam would be so good as to turn her face a little more toward the light."

The sphinx laughed again but she turned her face a little more toward Gregory.

"Such a wonderfully self-possessed model," murmured Gregory. "The pose is so natural."

"Sphinxes have had a good deal of practice at posing," observed the sphinx. "It's one of the things we do while asking riddles."

"Ah, yes" murmured Gregory, "to be sure. Riddles. Your Ladyship asked some very clever riddles. That one about the legs. Very witty. I don't believe I could have guessed it."

"It puzzled a number of people," said the sphinx, "though the solution always struck me as obvious. After all, what else could the answer have been?"

"To be sure," said Gregory. "Quite so." He was painting away and hardly heard what the sphinx had said. He didn't care about the answer to the riddle.

"But what was the answer?" asked Caspar. He loves riddles and jokes. "And for that matter, what was the riddle?"

"Go back to the world and find out," said the sphinx.

"Oh, we can't go back now," said Caspar. "We haven't seen Hy Breasil yet."

162

"Are you quite sure you want to go there?"

"Oh, quite," said Fox. "We have to go there. We must find out who called Guelph."

"In other words," said the sphinx, "you have reached the beginning of your journey."

"The beginning!" I exclaimed. "But we've been all over the centuries. We've been in courts and deserts and rushing from one time to the end of it."

"When you reach the beginning," said the sphinx, "you will know who called. It was the call that set you on the journey, was it not?"

"But if we get to the beginning," said Fox, "when shall we ever see the end of it?"

"For all you know," said the sphinx, "the end may lodge in the beginning."

"Eternity is a snake with its tail in its mouth," said Brother Hedgehog, dipping his brush in a smear of gold paint. "Ah, that is better. The mane of the sphinx is threaded with gold. One cannot have too much gold paint."

"There is always enough gold paint in Hy Breasil, Gregory," said the sphinx. She turned her gaze on me. To return the gaze of the sphinx was like looking directly into the sun and I squinted at her through my eyelashes.

"You may enter Hy Breasil," said the sphinx, "but

you must give your solemn word that you will not remain there."

"Of course we won't remain," I said. "We intend to see it and go home."

"You might wish to remain," said the sphinx, "but you must leave when the time comes."

"But how shall we know that time?"

"You will be told. Now enter and find the beginning. Gather your horses and leap the Straits."

José and Caspar crouched over their horses' necks. I did the same and felt Fox tighten her arms about my waist. I set Guelph to a canter and felt the wind in my face as he gained speed. Guapo raced along with us, his ears streaming in the wind. Guelph rose under us like a wave up and up — I thought we must be over the moon — and the next instant he came to ground, light as a butterfly.

We were in the courtyard of a castle. Above us gleamed turrets and battlements. Banners fluttered in the warm breeze and from every tower bells were chiming. Cathedral towers glimmered through the watery air. Our horses cantered across the courtyard and through the castle gates into a great hall whose vaulted ceiling arched over us, the color of dawn. We pulled our steeds to a halt and dismounted. The hall was hushed and fragrant, but from somewhere I heard music — the same music that I had caught in snatches on our journey. It was faint but not far, almost as though it were inside my own head.

"It's our very own castle," said Fox, in a breathless whisper. "But now we're inside it. We built it this afternoon on the beach. How did it get here?"

"It was here all the time," said Guelph. "It is you that have moved. It looks out on all time and space. Look out the windows and you will see the whole world and all its history."

I moved to one of the lancet windows to look. Guelph was right. From one window I could see the dinosaur heave his bulk from the slime and from another I saw the first man bring fire from an angry mountain. I saw stone change to bronze, and bronze to steel. Huge dogs howled from the great wall of China. Carthaginian elephants trampled Alpine snows on their way to Rome. Temples rose and fell like waves. I saw the palace gardens in Madrid where our princess fondled Guapo in the shade of an orange tree. I saw the shadow of the Grand Inquisitor. Our princess was an empress beside the banks of a great river and her empire stretched as far as the Straits of Anian. I turned from a window, dazzled, and heard Fox and Caspar running from window to window, shouting to each other.

"What have you in yours? I've got William the Conqueror. Look at that red beard! I can see the Battle of Hastings. Oh, poor King Harold! And off there in the distance I can see Runnymede. Oh, there's King John, under the oak."

"And there's Marco Polo! He's talking to the Great Khan. It's Kubla Khan. Imagine seeing Kubla Khan. What will they say at school when I tell them? They won't believe me — there is Cortez, General Washington — but it's all true. There is our Mission, our own Mission San Carlos and the Royal Road."

I turned from a window to move to another and saw, standing beside me, the infanta of our adventure in the garden. She was standing on tiptoe, fluttering her fan, peeping through the window which I was just leaving. Guapo sat at her feet, panting after his long leap into Hy Breasil.

"What are you doing here?" I said to the infanta. I was so surprised to see her standing beside me that I forgot the "Your Highness" bit.

"I've as good a right to be here as you," she said. "After all, it's my childhood too. And José's. That was a nasty trick you played, taking him with you and leaving me behind. But I finally got here. It's lovely, isn't it. What a pity it can't last."

It was the childhood of the whole world in which

we stood. Hy Breasil, lost beneath the waves of Anian, was the mansion we built which everyone — dwarf and dog, priest and princess and pauper — must leave behind him. It was here that all past years were gathered. That was why the sphinx had told us we could not stay.

"I have to stay," I said, "until we find out who called Guelph."

"That is simple," said a voice. "It's all in the play. You have only to go to the play. I called."

I looked around the luminous hall with its enormous freight of years. My grandmother, the gypsy queen, in purple and gold stood amongst them, looking down at me laughing. "Tell your fortune, little gentleman?"

"So it was you all the time," I said. She tossed her head and the sea light gleamed in her red hair.

"Don't tell me you're surprised," she said. "I thought you might have guessed."

"I couldn't possibly have guessed," I said. "Does Guelph know?"

"I know now," said Guelph. "And I can't say that it comes as any real surprise. I am, after all, an experienced unicorn. But in pursuit of the ends one occasionally loses sight of the means. The purpose of your summons, Madam, is obscure to me."

"The children needed you," said our grandmother. "And we have a play in hand. Only you can make the play be. It may surprise you, Guelph, but your species is exceedingly rare these days. Hardly anyone has seen a unicorn lately."

"That's right." It was Caspar. "You were the very first we ever saw. We needed you but Balthasar needed you more — to get back to the sea. And Black Beauty needed to be a real horse, even though he doesn't like it much. Remember what you told us. Guelph, about lost causes and blighted hopes?"

"But it wasn't only that," I said. "Everyone needed the unicorn. Everyone we saw. He brought Gregory to the beasts and he brought us all together."

"Yes," said our grandmother. "And he must part you."

"Oh no," we all cried. I heard our voices, an enormous chorus. "We want to stay here. We don't want to go."

"You are only at the beginning of the journey," said our grandmother sternly.

"I want to stay here," cried Velazquez's princess. "I don't want to be Empress of Austria."

"I do not want to be a cardinal of Spain," cried José.

"I want to stay and be with Balthasar and Guapo," said Fox. "Why should I grow up?"

"And what about Black Beauty?" exclaimed Caspar. "I don't want to grow up either. If I grow up, I shan't be able to ride Black Beauty."

"How will you ever know how wonderful it was if you stay?" said our grandmother. "To possess Hy Breasil you must leave it. Balthasar is in the sea. You won't lose him. Black Beauty runs in the paddock. And Brother Hedgehog will paint his beasts a thousand times for you, but you cannot stay here. You must return to earth in order to remember it all. Out — before you go mad."

She stood there under the pearly dome, majestic and terrible as the sphinx, pointing us out into the other world. She was the sphinx. She was Fox's gypsy queen and the eagle who had snatched the serpent from the rock in the desert. She was the beginning of our journey. She had given us our childhood. And now she was making us leave it.

"No," we cried. "We want to stay."

"Back!" she cried. "Back, the way you came."

The great shape of the sphinx seemed to engulf her. The gryphons and the hippogriffs, the mermaids and the dolphins, the centaurs and sirens rose up before us, magical and menacing. "Go!" they cried. "Go. Before you must remain forever."

They advanced on us, a terrible phalanx, the vanguard of nightmare. "Go to the end of the journey."

"They are right," I heard Guelph's voice silvery under their cacophony. "And they are dangerous." They were coming closer now, claw and wing and terrible shining eyes.

"Help us, oh help us!" It was José. He had known the danger all along.

"Give me the words of power," implored Guelph.

I shouted the words at the top of my lungs.

✦✦✦ TEN ✦✦✦✦✦✦

IT WAS NO USE trying to finish the castle. The wind was too much for us and cold water was swirling in, filling the moats and carrying away the bridges. It was time to go home. We left our creation reluctantly to the sea.

Our grandparents were out. They had left a note saying that they were at a dress rehearsal and that we were to eat our supper and go to bed. We followed instructions and ate what was laid out on the table, melons and figs and cold ham. We were unaccountably depressed and sleepy. We even went to bed without being told.

I woke early the next morning. It was almost frighteningly clear when I opened the blind. If the earth hadn't curved, you could have seen the coast of China and all the islands in between. I could see jays and orioles darting in and out among shiny leaves of the cumquat tree under my window. It was the kind of day that ought to have been one of our best; it was the day of our grandmother's play.

As it turned out, it happened to be one of Caspar's days. His days seem to befall him without his being able to do anything much about them. At nine o'clock one of the cats, a skinny ginger one, with a trusting disposition, allowed itself to fall into his hands. He bandaged it with scotch tape. Conchita came in with the ironing and rescued the cat. She had to cut the scotch tape off and remove the unmanageable bits with alcohol. It was an awful job and Conchita got scratched. This made things worse because Caspar wasn't scratched at all. Conchita gave a long sermon on kindness to animals, citing the Blessed Saint Francis.

At ten o'clock he cleaned his tennis shoes with library paste. He hadn't read the label and he had thought it was white shoe polish.

At eleven o'clock he went through his bureau drawers and his closet and threw away all the things he didn't want — all his underclothes, socks, pajamas, and his toothbrush. He threw them in the incinerator so there was no getting them back.

At half-past eleven he cut all the buttons off his

blazer to make wheels for a wagon he was building out of a matchbox.

At twelve o'clock he ate lunch — in his room.

At one o'clock, after a short rest, he tied all the furniture in the big room together with string and then crisscrossed it like a spider's web.

At two o'clock our grandfather found out about it by walking unawares into the room, tripping over the string and pulling over on top of himself two chairs, a cake stand, and a Chinese table complete with a Buddha, and a vase of roses.

At ten minutes past two our grandfather beat Caspar.

Our grandmother said it was foolish to beat the boy. He would only learn not to tie furniture together and think of something worse instead.

Our grandfather said that sometimes it was fun to do foolish things.

Caspar said that beating children was against the law, and our grandfather said that it was legal in a private residence.

At three o'clock adult displeasure had washed over Fox and me, innocent though we were, and we were told to go out of doors and stay out of doors with the following restrictions. We were to let the horses alone until Esteban was free to come riding with us. We were not to dig holes in the lawn or pick any flowers. We were not to put any bandages on anything, human or otherwise; we were not to glue or tie anything to anything else; we were to dispose of no property, and we were not to get in any fights with strangers.

"Suppose we get in a fight with someone we know," said Caspar. Our grandfather told him not to be impertinent.

"It makes me wonder," said Caspar, when our grandfather was out of earshot, "why we came here at all."

"We came for a vacation," said Fox, "you know, to have fun."

"But I'm not having fun."

"Well, you will. There's the play tonight. And if you can stay out of trouble, we might even get to it."

"I'm hungry," said Caspar, as though announcing something very surprising, such as the sudden arrival of a giraffe or the birth of triplets.

"You can't be. You had lunch."

"It wasn't much of a lunch. And besides, I've been beaten since then. It made me hungry."

"We can go to the orchard and eat oranges," I said. So we did. After this stormy morning the peaceful atmosphere of the orchard was very welcome. We all surrendered to daydreams and speculated about the play. I rather liked the idea of a play out of doors with Point Lobos and the night sky for scenery. I had a feeling it would be something quite out of the ordinary.

When the sun was hanging over the Point we judged that perhaps all was forgiven and that we could return to the house without fear of retribution. We ventured in the kitchen door in an apologetic sort of way and found our grandmother dressing a dish of artichokes.

"Well," she cried, "are you ready for tonight?"

We said of course we were.

"Are you in the leading part?" asked Fox.

"Not the leading part," said our grandmother, "but one suitable to my talents."

"What is the play?" asked Fox.

"It isn't really a play. It's a masque, more a pageant than a play. It's about this place."

"Where is it going to be?" I asked.

"In a glade outside the village. It's a charity thing."

"Charity for who?" asked Caspar.

"If you don't approve of the cause you can stay home," said our grandmother.

"Oh, I'm always for charity," said Caspar. "I believe in being nice to people."

"This isn't even for people. It's for mountain lions and bears and redwood trees."

"I'll come," said Caspar firmly. "I love bears and mountain lions. Is it for seals, too?"

"Seals and sea otters and giant turtles."

"Good," said Caspar. "I like that. When's supper?"

"You can have it now, if you wish. And you can have another one after the play. There will be a celebration."

"Who will be there?" I asked.

"Everyone," replied our grandmother. "Everyone you can think of. And you had better eat now so you can be dressed in plenty of time. I must go now. Your grandfather will take you, but he is playing in the orchestra. You must come with the music."

Our grandmother had made us a meal of abalone chowder served right in the shells, and grapes and nectarines.

We ate in a state of pleasurable anticipation and relief that Caspar's day had almost run its course.

This was to be Caspar's first experience at the theater and he was rightly very much excited by the whole occasion. He dressed himself with what our grandfather described as truly foppish taste and borrowed some My Sin from our grandmother's dressing table.

"She'll never miss a spoonful or two," he said, pouring it on his head. Obviously his day was not quite over. He smelled very strong but he looked quite handsome in his gray flannels and blue blazer, even though the buttons were off.

We drove out past the Mission, all gold in the setting sun. The ocean lay under a wall of purple cloud which reared up from the horizon like a great wave about to break.

"Where are the Straits of Anian?" asked Caspar.

"They wash the shores of Hy Breasil," replied our grandfather glibly. "And don't ask me where that is. It's where the Atlantic and the Pacific mingle their waters, perhaps. The Spaniards thought it might be somewhere near here. While they were looking for it they found Mexico, Santa Barbara, San Francisco, and Monterey, which they missed several times. But they never found the Straits. They never found Hy Breasil either. They finally gave up looking for them. They decided that they didn't exist. I told you at breakfast that this was probably the reason that they were never found."

"That was rather silly," said Caspar. "If people

decided that everything they couldn't find didn't exist, nobody would ever find anything. Why, nobody would ever have a toothbrush or a baseball glove or any lesson books. When I've lost things they turn up right under my nose. My mother finds them as easily as anything and they don't stop existing at all. Perhaps the Straits of Anian are right here somewhere, only we don't have the sense to see them."

"That is of course a possibility," said our grandfather. "And it's certainly true that anyone can spend a lifetime looking for his spectacles while all the time they're on his forehead. If he would only wear them on his nose where they belong, he'd see them at once. Or, on the other hand, he might miss them entirely. There'd be no point in finding them if they were where they ought to be."

"Are the Straits of Anian where they ought to be? And Hy Breasil?" asked Caspar.

"Well, they're not where I can find them easily, so the chances are that they're where they ought to be," said our grandfather. "If you're really determined to find the Straits of Anian, ask yourself, 'where would I be if I were the Straits of Anian?'"

"If I were the Straits of Anian," said Fox, "I should be right here. Because that's where I am."

"I should say you are," said our grandfather. "You

could be detected for miles around. You should learn restraint with the perfume bottle."

"I haven't used a drop of perfume. I smell like that naturally."

"My dear girl!" exclaimed our grandfather.

"It's me," said Caspar softly. "I think it's lovely. And if I were the Straits of Anian I'd be where our castle is."

"Our castle's too small for that," I said. "It would be flooded."

"Perhaps the Straits are tiny," said Caspar.

"The fathers who built the Royal Road of the missions thought they might turn up any time," said our grandfather. "Of course they never did. If they had, they might have prevented Fray Serra from building the road and finding all the other things he was looking for — this place, among others. Perhaps if you start looking for something else instead, you'll run across them."

"I'll try," said Caspar. "What's the best thing to look for when you're looking for something else?"

"You've got me there," said our grandfather. "I was looking for peace and quiet when I met your grandmother."

"What did you get instead?" asked Fox.

"Well, I got her. And you."

"Now isn't that better than a lot of dull peace and quiet?" asked Fox.

"Well, I'm learning to live with it."

He turned the car inland and left the sea behind in the fading light. We drove toward the darkening hills among cypresses twisting in the dusk and came at last to the glade, where a semicircle of live oaks formed a natural stage. The headlights of the car flooded the grove with light as we drove in. For a moment the grove was twice as real, twice as much a theater as it had been when it was in shadow. The darkness of the live oaks was like the darkness under the sea, and the smaller, lighter shrubbery was green as wet grass. There was a heavy smell of pine and pettisporum and it mingled with Caspar's My Sin and made me dizzy. Fox fanned herself and said, "Whew! Caspar, you really reek."

Our grandfather took us to the middle of a row of chairs, the folding kind with slats that are usually found in school auditoriums.

"Here I am quit of you," said our grandfather. "I shall now join the orchestra. Enjoy the play. Esteban will pick you up after the performance."

He disappeared, swallowed up by the grove of live oaks. I could hear faintly the sound of musicians tuning up offstage. From somewhere behind the gathering audience Esteban flickered his lights, flooding the stage in soft yellow light, then dimming it down to almost total darkness, save for one silvery spot showing one bough here or a cluster of bushes there.

All sorts of strange people came to this play; men in beards and sandals, and ladies in smocked blouses and wooden beads — the sort of people who love art and nature and higher things. Even the boy who had come to breakfast was there. He was taking tickets and telling people where to sit. Later, during the intermission, I saw him throwing dice in the wings. There was an old gentleman in white flannel trousers and a blue blazer who called me "young sir" — something you almost never hear these days. Brother Gregory was here, darting on and off the stage, adjusting lights with Esteban. Just before the play began he whisked himself into a chair and sat staring at the stage with an impatient waiting look. He was expecting to be taken somewhere, I thought. Fox, sitting beside me in her Paris dress, waved to someone in the bushes which served as wings for the stage. "That's Margaret Hapgood," she whispered. "She sees us." And she sat bolt upright as though she thought that Margaret could see her better that way.

Cars came up behind us, flashing their headlights on the greenery. They kept the grove in a constant state of change. It was never the same for two minutes together.

"I wish we could live like this always," breathed Fox. She was looking nice in her French dress. It is mauve with pale yellow ribbons at the shoulders, mini-skirted, and it suits her.

"It's part of the way we live," I whispered back. "But we'd want to be in the play, wouldn't we, not just always watching it." Then all the lights went down and for a moment the audience and the stage were entirely dark. Then the music sounded and the light of the masque began to dawn. It dawned on the deathbed of an old Spanish duchess, the Duchess of Borges. She was afraid for her soul and she sought a way to save it. She endowed a mission in the loneliest place in the world. The light of the masque fell upon the lonely monks at the Mission San Francisco de Borges at the beginning of the Royal Road.

Our grandmother spoke for the duchess:

The Borgia duchess, her last confession:
"Father, give all to the solitary:
Give to the glacier, give to the desert,
The tangled bush and the eagle's eyrie.

"Mad Don Carlos and grieving Philip
Mourn in the blaze of Castillian noondays.
The birds fly over the Mexican mountains,
White gods trample the burning Indies.

"Where do you go, Margarita Teresa?
The king grows old and the princes perish.
Eastern Empire, western wilderness,
The pearl bride and the trumpets' flourish.

"Woeful dwarf in silks and sorrow,
Simpering spaniel and questing warrior,
Indian supple as snake and simple
Raise me a church for a Gospel carrier.

"Leave the green grove where the citrons glow,
The scimitar shines in the Danube's ripple:
Stone against dust in the jaguar desert:
St. Francis rears the shard of a steeple.

"Where do you wander, sweet Father Juniper?
The palms of Mallorca are far and fragrant —
Feed my sheep and mark where my sandal
Prints the dust: my church is a vagrant.

"Raise Vera Cruz on the smoking altars,
Raise St. Clare to the poor in pity,
Saint Gabriel bringer of holy tidings,
Saint Louis, the bishop and Barbara's city.

"Chaste Inez and the Good Adventure,
Saint Michael, Saint John — the birds will nest there —

Quetzl, fly home to the white volcano —
Eagle and princess will find their rest there.

"Seek El Dorado and shining Anian,
Seek gold and pearl and youth's elixir.
Hy Breasil beckons, spirits are singing,
Briar Rose sleeps and Florian wakes her.

"The sea lion shouts to the singing chantry,
Above the cloister the whalebone whitens,
Steeped in brine and shell-encrusted,
The bells give back the sound of tritons.

"One point past the hithermost headlands,
One wave beyond the climbing comber —
Here the far country — the straits are shining,
Unicorns leap and dragons slumber — "

The pageant slipped by like a gigantic ribbon. Part
of me was watching it and part of me was in it.
The mad prince and the pale princess glided through
a pavane and gave place to the lonely monks, to the
bird out of the tower, to the deaths of kings, and the
long marches of their subjects.

There was a kind of terror to the masque. Mon-
sters and people moved under the lights, only half
embodied. The actors in their brave costumes were
parallel to us — near enough to touch almost, but of
another world. There was a barrier between actor and
audience which neither could cross without becom-

ing something other than they were. It was like the barrier between now and then — between life here and life somewhere else. Perhaps one of us wasn't real at all — our grandmother on the other side of the lights and the music — or us. The princess and the dwarfs and the priests and the soldiers or the lady next to Fox, keeping time to the music with her head and a palm-leaf fan.

I began to shake. Something marvelous had happened and I wasn't at all sure that I liked it. I felt as though I had been here all my life or for several lifetimes. I looked at Fox, sitting beside me, pretty as the King of Spain's daughter. Her lip trembled. She was going to cry. I suppose it was the poetry. Poetry has a funny way of doing that to you sometimes — especially when it is not in the least sad. And there was nothing sad about any of this masque. It was more a celebration than anything else. Nevertheless it was making Fox cry.

Our grandmother's voice streamed out in poetry, the poetry of the place we were in, and because we were unused to seeing what the poetry told us to see, it hurt us. Our grandmother was not our grandmother at all. She was merely the poetry and that hurt us too. The poetry and the music and the dancers seemed to be inside my head.

From down in the valley there came a long melodious whinny. Guelph tossed his glowing head in the moonlight. The words of power had come alive. As he had said, Guelph brooded over amateur theatricals and other lost causes.

After the masque there was a fine party in our grandmother's drawing room for all the actors, who were only people after all, eating their heads off. The dice-playing boy ate the most. I couldn't help mentioning to our grandmother after I had told her that I thought she was the best actress I had ever seen — which seemed to please her — that I was surprised when the play was over. It had seemed so real that I thought it was real life and that it would never end.

"It is your life," she said, "and someday it will end. But there is no *un*real life — and the play is just as real. It's a part of your life now."

I was glad to hear this. I should have hated to lose that play.

There was lovely food at the party, lobster in pastry shells and brandied peaches and little sausages, and we made that a part of us too, and also some champagne. It was rather nasty to taste and it made your ears ring. It rang Caspar straight to sleep. Somebody heaved him up from the sofa, where he lay curled up, and carried him to bed without waking him. It was Brother Gregory. I followed him upstairs, very sleepy myself. Brother Gregory put Caspar into his bed, put his finger to his lips and slipped out of the room. I went to my room and lay down on my bed, which rocked a little. I heard the waves breaking on the shore and the voices of people leaving the party. Then I slept so deeply that time stopped.

I woke to ripples of sunlight dancing across the ceiling through the slats of the blinds. I felt shaky and thirsty and cross and as though I had a lizard between my teeth. Fox came running into the room to tell me that the people who take care of redwood trees and mountain lions had made thousands of dollars.

"It's a marvelous day," she cried. "Do wake up. Esteban says we can ride the horses to the Point. I want to see the Mission. There's a brother there who paints pictures, the one who helped write the play. And that spaniel is still here. I've just fed him. Grandmother says he can stay if nobody claims him. Come *on,* Berkeley. We've been here three days and we've hardly seen a thing yet."

188

DATE DUE

NOV 1 1 1990			